WILL STEPP

1986

STORIES

Copyright © 2025 by Will Stepp
All rights reserved.

No part of this publication may be reproduced, stored or transmitted in any form or by any means, electronic, mechanical, photocopying, recording, scanning, or otherwise without written permission from the publisher. It is illegal to copy this book, post it to a website, or distribute it by any other means without permission.

ISBN 979-8-9915036-0-0

For my family

Grazing Field
1

New Knife
11

Mail Walk
27

Clubhouse
37

Drainage Pipe
53

Dog and Butterfly
65

Truck Stop
81

Blizzard
107

YMCA
115

2006
131

GRAZING FIELD

It was cool under the shade of the maple tree. Cooler, at least. The backyard was perfectly quiet except for a mild rustling of leaves overhead. The air smelled like a mixture of freshly cut grass and burnt engine oil. As I rested, cup of lemonade in hand, I chewed on a nugget of ice and admired my handiwork.

Our backyard was a pain to cut. It was frustrating to navigate the mower around all the ruts and mounds. Especially our mower, which would stall out if you so much as looked at it wrong. Despite the hassle, I thought I had done a fine job. My lines were straight, with no stray tufts of grass that I could see. All that remained to do was the hill behind our property. The hill led to a small horse pasture. I usually saved it for last, since it was such a bear to do.

The view of the pasture from our trailer was the main reason we moved to the trailer park, in February of that same year. At least, as far as me and my sister were concerned it was. I remember when the landlady was showing us around. She knelt beside Rachel and pointed up the hill. At the fence stood a beautiful mare, the color of sand.

My sister's eyes widened, and she tugged on my mother's coat.

"Horsey, Mama!"

My mother laughed.

"That's right, baby girl."

The landlady pulled an apple from her purse and asked if we wanted to feed the horse a snack. Of course! we told her. She then demonstrated how we should offer it. Flat on the palm, with arm outstretched. She told us the horse's name was Dusty, and to not be afraid, because the horse was gentle and loved children very much.

My sister and I approached the fence. As we neared, the horse saw us, snorted, and backed away. However, she must have smelled the fruit, because she then ambled over to where we stood. Rachel lost her nerve and dropped the apple on the ground, running back down the hill to our mother. I seized the moment and picked it back up, offering the fruit over the fence.

Dusty bared her teeth and nibbled a bite. Then another. And took a final bite that slobbered my palm, causing me to laugh.

Then she lowered her head and allowed me to stroke her mane. I shouted for my sister to come and pet the horse too, but she was chicken, hiding behind my mother's legs.

On the drive home that afternoon, my mother asked

us if we wanted to live there. My sister and I both shouted Yes! and we moved in shortly thereafter.

As I was about to nod off, I jolted awake and got to my feet. There was still work to be done and I was losing daylight. Then again, I was feeling lazy, so to procrastinate a bit longer I trekked up the hill for a look around.

The pasture was empty, but that was no surprise. We barely saw Dusty anymore. Now and then we'd see her off in the distance, head bowed to the Earth, munching on grass. But that was all we saw of her. I figured it was because we never had apples to give. Our family kept oranges and bananas, and she didn't seem to like those as much.

On the fence hung an old metal sign, painted white and stenciled with black letters.

NO TRESPASSING

I draped my arms over the fence and gazed across the field. On the other side of the field was a path that disappeared into the woods. From my vantage, it was impossible to tell where the path led, which fascinated me to no end.

The mower needed gas. On the way to fetch the can from the work shed, I passed by the kitchen window and saw inside. My mother was at the stove, stirring a pot of spaghetti sauce, while my sister lay on a blanket in the living room, sound asleep.

As I approached the mower, something kept drawing my eyes back to the hill. It was irresistible. Then, before I was even aware of what I was doing, I had dropped the can on the grass and was racing up the slope. When I reached the fence, I ducked between two of the rails and stood up on the other side, facing our property.

From this side of the fence, everything seemed farther away. Unfamiliar, even. I turned and faced the field. It was vast to my eyes, like an ocean of green. I took one step. Then another. And I was off.

At my feet were dandelions and thistles. I picked a dandelion and rolled it between my fingers, squeezing a milky sap from its broken stem. Sweat bees were hovering over the thistles, and I gave them a wide berth, hoping not to get stung.

Before I knew it, I was halfway across the field. Ahead of me was the path into the woods. Behind me was the fence at the back of our property, now merely a thin line. The trailer we lived in was completely out of view.

In the distance, I heard a peal of thunder.

It made no sense. The sky was blue, with hardly a cloud in sight. Despite that, my instinct was to find cover immediately. The only thing nearby was some rusted-out farming equipment, which looked as if it hadn't been maintained since before I was born.

More thunder.

Then I saw. In my periphery. Careening towards me at full gallop.

Dusty, the horse.

I broke into a sprint, headed for cover. The faster I ran, the further away everything seemed to get. From the thundering of hooves, I knew she must be right on top of me. In a flash of imagination, I saw her rear up on hind legs and come crashing down onto my fragile skull. I didn't dare look back. There was a narrow opening between two sections of the machinery. I wriggled inside like an earthworm and dropped to the ground, covering my head. As I lay there, bare-chested against the earth, I felt my heartbeat pounding.

It was quiet. But I knew she was there, waiting for me. Moments passed, and finally I steeled my nerves and rolled over. Staring back at me was a massive horse head, with two eyes like obsidian, the teeth bared. I scrambled backwards.

The ground was littered with machinery detritus. Nuts and bolts, a hollow cylinder, a bent spring. That gave me an idea. I picked up the cylinder and heaved it through the opening I had crawled through. The projectile spun in the air and landed with a thud some feet away. But it did the trick. The horse raised its head and side-stepped over to investigate. Then, gripping the frame with both hands, I silently wormed my way back through the opening. Once my feet hit the ground, I darted towards the woods, arms and legs furiously pumping.

1986

The thunder returned. It was a critical moment. Either I would make it safely into the woods or be trampled to death. Nearly out of breath, I reached the tree line and dove into the brambles, ducking behind a tree overgrown with kudzu.

There I waited.

Dusty stamped at the edge of the woods for several minutes, huffing through her nostrils and flicking her tail, before seeming to lose interest in me altogether, and trotting away.

My heartbeat returned to its normal pace and I continued along the path. The ground was bedded with the remnants of leaves from the trees which towered overhead. The woods were so dense I could not see very far ahead. But soon, the trees grew sparser. I noticed a gap between the trees and picked up my pace. When I finally emerged, I found myself standing on the edge of a wide pond.

Nearby, a heron stood on one leg on the muddy bank. When it saw me, it ruffled its wings and took flight over the surface of the water. Then, just as it reached the opposite bank, it ascended above the treetops and disappeared from view.

Someone else was there.

On the other side.

A boy my age.

He wore cutoffs and sneakers, the same as me. I waved to him, but he didn't wave back. He just stood there, staring straight ahead. Maybe he lived nearby, I thought.

Maybe he came to fish in the pond. Either way, he was bound to know more about this place than me. And I wanted to know more.

I stomped through the tall grass around the perimeter of the pond until I reached a clearing on the other side. There was a grassy bank which turned to mud at the water's edge. But the boy was not there. Nor was there any evidence that he had been there. That seemed impossible to me, as the ground was so soft.

I investigated the woods around the clearing. There was no path leading into it. Then I headed down the bank. The surface of the pond reflected an inverted world of inverted trees and a sky-dome which rippled in the breeze.

A strange feeling came over me. That all of this had happened before. That everything was repeating. I predicted a thing, and in the next moment, that thing happened. The wavering of grass in the wind. The skittering of an insect across the water. The smacking of an acorn into a branch as it fell from a nearby tree. All was foretold by me. All happened as it was foretold. That was why I was not surprised when I saw myself emerge from the path on the other side of the pond. And was not surprised when I waved at me. Because I had walked that path before.

Countless times before.

And fled from Dusty. And crossed the field. And mowed the lawn on a Sunday afternoon. And moved into the trailer park with my mother and sister. And stayed with my grandparents after my father left us in Ohio. And

1986

moved back to Georgia with all our possessions loaded into a U-Haul trailer. And stood at the top of the stairs in the old farmhouse, when I should have been asleep, listening to my parents argue. And, earlier that same day, tripped over a stump in the front yard, scraping my knee, and destroying the balsa wood airplane I had built with my father at the kitchen table. And explored the cornfield next to the farmhouse. And stumbled terrified into a spider web, with its maker, a black and gold orb weaver, resting in the center.

    Spiders had existed three hundred million years before human beings, or so I read in a library book. Before the dinosaurs even. After the first animals had emerged from the oceans for survival. When the Earth was different, covered with ancient plant life and bizarre amphibious creatures. When the continents were breaking up and colliding, forming mountain ranges which still exist to this day. Before which time all the landmasses of the Earth were together in a formation called Pangaea. When the world was covered with water. Before which time was all molten rock and toxic gasses. When asteroids impacted the surface of the planet. Celestial bodies from where we do not know and can only speculate. From Mercury, Venus, and Mars. Or from interstellar bodies, which may have fallen into the orbit of our sun. The sun, which is the star at the center of the solar system, formed by an accumulation of dust and gas, which eventually collapsed under its own gravity and began to burn. Millions of years before the formation of Earth. Those particles, originating from an explosion at the beginning of time itself. And—

A faint echo stirred me from my reverie. It was my mother's voice. Calling me from the back porch, as she often did when it was suppertime and I was off somewhere.

I became aware of my surroundings. It was like no time had passed at all. The late afternoon sun was shining over the treetops, while the ghost of a crescent moon was rising in the eastern sky.

I took one final look at the secret pond I had discovered in the woods beyond the grazing field, and then retraced my steps and eventually found my way home.

NEW KNIFE

My mother entered through the front door wearing a pink coat, her breath visible from the cold. She clasped two frozen hands onto my cheeks and planted a warm kiss on my forehead.

"We're off to the flea market, sweetie," she said. "Mind Grandpa till we get back."

"Okay," I mumbled, barely awake.

"For breakfast, there's a pan of sausage and biscuits on the stove. Or you can have cereal," she said, adding when my eyes widened, "but not Froot Loops."

"Okay."

"What's that look for?"

"Nothing."

"Better not be."

She and my grandmother left for the flea market, while I ate breakfast alone at the kitchen table.

*

1986

Just as I finished washing off my dishes in the sink, my grandfather came through the carport door, carrying a toolbox and whistling a tune. He told me he needed my help in the basement. A hose on the washing machine had sprung a leak, and it was going to be a two-man job to fix it. Or, maybe he didn't want me sitting on my butt watching Saturday morning cartoons while he did all the chores. That was my guess.

Downstairs, my grandfather flipped on an old light switch and a series of fluorescent lights flickered on. They illuminated both the main room and a storage room in the back, where my grandmother kept her antique collection.

The washer and dryer were in the main room, along with a workbench scattered with tools, rags, and old coffee tins filled with bits and bobs. Also in the main room was a door that went out to the patio. Hanging around the doorknob was a string of bells, serving as a makeshift security alarm. And next to the door was a rusted-out trash can, filled with dog food for Ol' Red, a dearly beloved bird dog who had succumbed to cancer before I was born, and was buried in a sunken grave in the backyard.

My grandfather handed me the toolbox. Then he got down on all fours and crawled between the dryer and washing machine. There was much grunting and groaning, until finally the washing machine scraped a few inches in my direction.

A hand reached out.

"Flashlight."

I gave it over.

More grunting. Then a sigh.

Again, the hand.

"Screwdriver."

As he worked, my attention drifted to the workbench. I ran my hand along the tops of the tools and coffee tins, pretending it was a dirt bike jumping over hills. Next, I wandered into the antique room, which was one of my favorite places in the house.

It was a medium-sized room, with three hand-built wooden tables in the center and shelving along the walls. These shelves overflowed with relics of Americana. To my eyes, it all seemed entirely random and magical to explore.

A tin horse carousel next to a set of Native American bookends next to the remains of a Kellogg wall phone next to a tarnished shoehorn. And that was just the first table. By the time I reached the third, I had entered a different timeline altogether. Or rather, a place that had no concept of time, a kaleidoscope of human artifacts, all treasures for me to discover.

A finger whistle pierced my eardrums.

I snapped back to reality and rushed into the main room. My grandfather had crawled out and was scowling at me. When I stood before him, he jabbed a finger at the toolbox, at the new hose sitting on top.

"Hand it here."

I did so.

"Lookie son," he said.

1986

I looked at him.

"When you tell a man you'll be there for him, you gotta be there for him. Not fiddle-fartin around in the antique room. Savvy?"

"Yes, sir."

He roughed my hair as if to say no hard feelings. Then he took the hose, put the screwdriver between his teeth, and disappeared once again behind the washing machine. Moments later he was cursing. Turned out the new hose was too long.

His hand appeared, fingers waggling.

"You there?"

"Yes, sir."

"Good. Now listen. Fetch me something to cut this hose with. Bound to be something on the workbench, shelves, somewhere. Don't matter what it is, as long as it cuts."

"Okay."

I was determined to find the perfect tool for the job. What I hoped to find was a utility blade, something to slice through that hose like butter. But there wasn't anything like that on the workbench. The longer it took, the more I started to panic. Like I was taking too long. Like I was about to get yelled at again. Then, I remembered something that had momentarily caught my eye in the antique room.

A little green pocketknife.

It had two blades, one large and one small, halfway extended to lock, rusted there since God knows when. The

NEW KNIFE

handle was made from an emerald acrylic, pearlescent, now faded. The only other marking was a metal crest on the front. The crest was encrusted with rust bubbles, telling of further corruption within.

I brought the knife to him. He fought to open the blade, but it must have done the trick, because the next thing I was handed was a cut portion of hose, and then the knife. My grandfather came out, grinning at me. He wiped both hands on his pants and smoothed back his hair, noticing me as I regarded the knife.

"Good knife you found there," he said. "Old sucker, but she got the job done."

I nodded, working the rusted blades back and forth.

"Can I keep it, Grandpa?"

He frowned, not eager to disappoint.

"That blade's too rusty. You'll catch tetanus and your mama will have my behind."

"What's tetanus?"

"Lockjaw. Disease spread through the soil and whatnot. You know what that is."

He bared his teeth like a dog.

I said nothing.

"You never heard of lockjaw?"

"No."

"No? What the hell they teaching in school these days?"

I shrugged. "I don't know. Boring stuff."

He laughed. "Well shit, I guess some things never change."

1986

He held out his hand and I helped him to his feet. Then I returned the knife to the shelf in the antique room and we headed upstairs.

"Come on, hoss," he said. "Let's go scare up some cheese and crackers."

That afternoon I rode my bike through the neighborhood. The day was overcast, but not very cold. Wind caressed my face as I flew down the hill at the intersection of Doncaster and Pembroke, modulating my speed with the brakes. There was a sharp bend at the bottom of the hill, where both bicycles and cars had skidded off the road. But not me.

A few blocks after the bend was a two-way stop. Going left went to a cul-de-sac where my friend Noah lived. His was a red brick house with white shutters. The inside of his house always smelled like stewed carrots, which grossed me out, but what could I do? He was my friend.

I ditched my bike in their front yard and knocked on the carport door. Noah's dad greeted me, bleary-eyed and Budweiser in hand. He thumbed me towards the bedroom hallway, then returned to a football game on the television.

Noah was sitting on the floor playing Nintendo. Beside him were a couple of rental cases from the local video store. He acknowledged me with a nod, but his eyes never left the game he was playing. On the screen was a boss I knew he had never reached before.

Over the next few minutes, I patiently watched as he

got his ass handed to him. When the Game Over text scrolled into view, I couldn't help but grin.

He tossed the controller on the floor. "I can't beat that son of a bitch."

"That's because you suck," I said. "Give me that and I'll show you how it's done."

He rolled his eyes, handing me the controller. "I may suck at Mega Man, but you know what you suck at?"

I knew what he was going to say, so ignored the question. "Your problem is you need the air weapon. Crash Man is weak to air."

Noah contorted backwards and pulled a long cardboard box from underneath the bed. Inside was all kinds of candy, chocolate, bubble gum, plastic keychains, and packs of collectible cards. He rifled through the pile until he found a Whatchamacallit, offering it to me since he knew I liked them. But I declined.

"Could go for some Starburst."

"Out of those."

"I don't know then. What about Skittles?"

He went through the box but came up short.

"Out."

I paused the game and raised an eyebrow. Noah shrugged, understanding my concern.

"Time for a refill?"

We both agreed it was. It had been almost a month since our last refill. Therefore, after we got bored playing video games, we set off to the Rock Store, a nearby

1986

gas station and convenience store that sold a little bit of everything. It sat on the corner of a lot which also contained a BBQ joint, a consignment shop for baby clothes, and the Army Surplus Store.

On the way, I told Noah all about the green pocketknife, how cool it was, and how I wished my grandfather would have let me keep it.

"It would be so awesome to carry a pocketknife," he agreed, adding, "and useful too."

"I know."

Something occurred to him, and he raised a finger.

"You know, the Army store has all kinds of knives. In a display case out front."

We exchanged glances.

"I wonder if it's open today."

Behind the counter sat an obese man wearing a faded Don't Tread On Me t-shirt underneath a green army jacket. The sleeve on the side of his amputated arm was pinned near the shoulder. As we entered the building, he lifted his eyes from a crossword puzzle and nodded without a smile.

Noah split off from me, as we had planned. His task was to head down the aisle to the corner of the store most distant from the front counter. I hung back near the entrance, pretending to be interested in the table of camouflage pants, all while doing recon on the knife display case, which sat next to the cash register. The good news was the knives were not locked up. They were resting on a black velvet pad out in the open. It was perfect.

One knife in particular stood out from the others, a serrated edge blade with a textured black handle. It was the coolest knife I had ever seen. An orange price tag hung around it. Twenty-seven dollars and fifty cents.

Good Lord, I thought. It would take me forever to save up that much.

Noah shouted to the clerk, also as planned.

"Excuse me, sir?" he said. "Do you guys have any beef ravioli? That's the only MRE my dad likes, and I don't see any."

The clerk sighed. He heaved off the stool, pulling up his jeans as he ambled down the aisle, slow as a walrus.

That was my cue.

Careful not to draw attention to myself, I inched towards the display case. When I was close enough, I swiped a knife I had my eye on, and shoved it into my pocket, never breaking my stride. Then I wandered towards the camping gear and flipped through a spinning magazine rack, as nonchalant as I could be.

A few minutes later, I felt a presence standing behind me. A firm hand clasped my shoulder, and a shudder went through me.

"Hey dude," Noah whispered. "You ready to go?"

I really was.

Outside, we kept our heads down until we reached the back of the building. Our bikes were propped against the wall. Noah watched me with an expectant smile. Without saying a word, I climbed onto my bike and pedaled away. He followed behind.

"Let's go to the park!" I yelled over my shoulder.

There were two playgrounds at Etowah Park. The newer one was beside the entrance. It was the most popular. The older one was at the top of a winding hillside, partially dilapidated and obscured by pine trees. I always liked the older one more because it was secluded and none of the other kids ever played there.

We propped our bikes against a metal slide whose steps were rusted through and overgrown with lichen. I pulled the knife from my pocket and held it aloft as if it were Excalibur, the orange tag still dangling from its side. Noah's eyes grew wide.

"Best loot ever!"

He wanted to hold it, so I let him. While he practiced folding the blade and flicking it open with one hand, I found a small branch at the base of a nearby tree.

"See if you can slice through this."

He sized up the branch and gripped the knife for action.

"Hold it out," he said, "don't want to cut you."

I did so, as far from my body as possible.

"Ready?"

I nodded.

He brandished the knife overhead, hesitating for only a moment, and brought it down with all his might, splitting the wood into equal halves.

"Nice."

Over the next hour we came up with all sorts of challenges. We tossed enormous pinecones into the air and sliced them before they hit the ground. We practiced digging a hole in the red clay, or at least breaking it up nicely. We discovered that because it had a serrated edge, it was good for sawing anything that was too big to slice, if it ever came down to that.

"This is like the perfect knife to take on a hike in the woods."

"Or on a camping trip."

"Definitely."

It was an unspoken fact that the knife was mine, since I was the one who had taken the risk. For that reason, Noah asked my permission anytime he wanted to try something that might damage or dull the blade. But he was my partner in crime as far as I was concerned, and he could use it however he wanted, until it was time to go home, that was.

Eventually, we ran out of things to do and fell to admiring it. To my eyes, the knife was an artifact of true beauty. Perhaps the most beautiful thing I had ever seen. It was almost like jewelry in its craftsmanship. Not a toy. It was a tool. And a weapon.

At a certain point, it dawned on me that I wouldn't be able to use the knife whenever I wanted, because of how I had acquired it. Upon that realization, my heart sank. I shared my disappointment with Noah, and we both contemplated the problem.

1986

"Wait a sec," he said, after a few minutes. "I just got a crazy idea."

He had my attention.

"What day is coming up soon? Like next weekend."

"Halloween?"

He looked at me like I was stupid. But I merely shrugged, not following.

"Your birthday."

"Oh," I said. "That's right, it is."

He could tell I was still not putting it together.

"And what do you get on your birthday?"

Just as I was going to respond, it finally hit me. "Ah."

He grinned. "I know, right?"

"Do you think it would work?"

"Let's think it through," he said. "I know where my mom keeps the wrapping paper, so I can wrap it up like a real birthday gift. We even have bows and crap."

"Cool."

"And my parents never come to your party. Remember, last time I just rode my bike over. Are you having a party at your grandparents' house, like last year?"

"I mean, I guess so."

"See? Perfect."

My birthday fell on Sunday.

In the morning, my sister and I played in a gigantic pile of leaves my grandfather had raked in the front yard.

When we came inside, breathless and rosy-cheeked, the house was filled with the sweet aroma of birthday cake still baking in the oven.

Over the next few hours, friends and family arrived for the party, and a pile of gifts accumulated on the table in the den. I kept wandering over there, delirious with curiosity, in between the chores my mother had set for me. Brush hair, wash face, clean room, and so on.

Pretty soon, the house was full of people. All the kids went outside to play hide and seek. As I stood in front of a tree, counting to ten, Noah pulled up on his bike holding a small, wrapped gift with a bow on it.

"Happy birthday, dude."

After a lunch of hamburgers and hot dogs, my mother brought out the cake. It was my favorite, yellow cake with chocolate frosting, decorated with sprinkles and a candle for every year since I was born. She lit the candles, and everyone sang Happy Birthday. I blew out the candles, and we were served cake and ice cream.

Finally, it was time for the gifts.

We gathered around the table in the den. I stood in front and picked out which gifts to open. Not to be conspicuous, I ignored the one I knew to be from Noah, pretending it was just another gift on the pile. I chose a few of the larger boxes, which turned out to be a board game, a soccer ball, and a knitted sweater from my aunt Lorraine.

When there were only a few gifts remaining, I reached

for the gift from Noah. To really sell it, I asked who it was from before opening.

"That one is from me," Noah said, perfectly innocent.

I unwrapped the package and opened the little cardboard box. The knife was inside. I held it up, so everyone could see. There were oohs and aahs from everybody.

"Badass knife!" my uncle said, giving me a thumbs up.

"Whoa," one of my other friends said. "That is awesome!"

My mother reached down and ran her finger along the blade. She glanced at me, and then Noah, a tad suspicious.

"What a beautiful knife," she said, "but we're gonna have some rules. This is not a toy."

"Mom, I know."

The knife was mine.

All my friends were jealous, I could tell. Noah merely grinned, satisfied that our plan had worked. I placed the knife back in the box and set it on the table. It was the best gift of the day, no contest. I couldn't wait to play with it outside, so I opened the remaining gifts as quickly as possible.

One left was a small gift, wrapped in burlap, and tied with a piece of twine. I loosened the knot and unraveled the cloth. It was not even in a box. Just lying there. The little green pocketknife. It had been meticulously cleaned since the last time I saw it. All the rust had been removed, and the mechanism oiled. The blade itself, though still tarnished, had been both polished and sharpened. Someone had put a lot of care into its restoration. That was plain to see.

There was not much reaction to the old knife, after the new one. Everyone seemed to be thinking the same thing, but nobody said anything, out of politeness.

I looked at my grandfather, who was standing in the back. He was just staring ahead at nothing and wouldn't make eye contact with me.

"Thank you, Grandpa."

"Well," he answered, giving a half-hearted smile. His voice trailed off, and he didn't say much else the rest of the afternoon.

All that night I couldn't sleep. My mind was turning over images of my grandfather sitting at his workbench, wearing those magnifying glasses, as he restored the pocketknife for me. Carefully sanding the rust away. Gently wiping away the years of grime. Tenderly smiling as he imagined the delight on my face when I finally unwrapped the gift. My heart felt sick.

In the darkness, on the dresser, I could see the shadow of the box that contained the new knife. To even look at it made me want to throw up. I turned to face the wall, but it was still there in my mind's eye. And in the morning, it would be there. It was inescapable. What I had done could not be undone.

Outside the window, I saw the stars over the treetops.

1986

How innocent they seemed to me. Somehow their light revealed my wickedness, by contrast. It felt that way. Those fiery orbs had never known this feeling as they burned a million light-years away. Somehow, they were free and I was not.

I climbed down from the top bunk. My sister Rachel was sound asleep in the lower bunk, so I was careful not to wake her. Taking the box, I crept down the hallway to the kitchen, and then descended the steps to the basement.

When I reached the door to the patio, I carefully opened it, one inch at a time, to make sure the security bells wouldn't jangle. Then I was outside, under the stars, in the freezing cold. I crossed the yard, barefooted, feeling my way through the grass.

At the back of the yard was a small group of oak trees, separating our property from the neighbors, a kind of no-man's land. The ground was thick with old leaves and fallen branches.

There I knelt and dug with both hands. The earth was cold, and my hands hurt after only a minute. But I kept digging, and when the hole was deep enough, I placed the box containing the new knife within it and buried it there, in the backyard, where it would remain forever.

MAIL WALK

"Mom!" I said.

"I'm making popcorn, what do you need?"

"Rachel farted on my back."

"What?"

"She farted, on my back, when she was riding me around the living room."

A pause.

"Give me a minute."

Several minutes later, my mother re-entered the living room, carrying a red bowl of popcorn. I stood there, arms crossed, glaring at her.

"Well," I demanded, "what are you going to do about it?"

"What do you mean, what am I going to do about it?"

"My sister farted on my back and you're not going to do anything about it. That figures."

"And what exactly am I supposed to do about it, son?"

I threw up my hands.

"I don't know, something," I said, gesturing towards my sister. "Look! She's laughing at me."

Rachel somersaulted around the living room, giggling like a deranged orangutan.

"She's not laughing at you, honey. She's just laughing. She's only four. Relax."

"You always take her side."

My mother tried reasoning with me.

"Well, what happened? Why was she on your back in the first place?"

I explained, "Because, she was pretending to be a cowgirl and asked me to be her horse. And I'm okay with that. But I'm not okay with her farting on my back. Girls aren't supposed to do things like that."

"Well, I don't know if that's true."

"There you go again, taking her side."

Exasperated, my mother set the bowl on the coffee table and held her forehead.

"Look just go check the mail, okay honey? A walk will do you good. And while you're gone, I'll talk to Rachel. And when you get back, we can finish the game and watch the movie like we planned. Okay?"

"Fine."

I grabbed the mail key off the hook and left, slamming the door behind me.

*

MAIL WALK

Buncha bullshit. My sister is a freakin brat. I wish she was never born. And my mom. Her most of all. Dragging us to these crappy apartments just so she can be close to her precious job in the city. What about me? What about what I wanted? I was happy living at Nana and Grandpa's house. I was happy with my friends. And my school. Not that she cares about that. She's an asshole! Great, now I'm lost. Dead end. Parked cars. Where's the green electrical box? Where am I? Okay, don't panic. Remember the way back. Go right. Then left. And straight ahead until another left. Then you should see the mailbox across the wooden bridge. Go back to the beginning. Start over. All these buildings look the same. Same white, same corridor through the middle. I never liked it here from day one. The kids are mean. They make fun of the way I talk. At the playground, Kai Palmer threw a shingle at me and cut open my forehead. Everyone laughed. I remember. Blood running down my face. Might take stitches, the neighbor said. All because of her. Now she has the nerve to defend Rachel. Takes her side always. Against me. My sister gets to fart on whoever she wants, I guess. Little Miss Perfect. Whatever. I know better. She's just a brat. She goes in my Lego box even though she knows she's not supposed to. Broke the rocket ship I've been working on since before Thanksgiving. And I know she ate Lando Calrissian's helmet and then lied about it. Turn left here. Now straight. This place is like a maze, I swear to God. I hate it so much. Where am I? Keep going. Should have

1986

worn a jacket. It's colder than a witch's titty out here. Haha. Goosebumps on my arm. Why do we get those, I wonder? And why are they called goosebumps? Why not duckbumps? Or turkeybumps? Turkey sandwich. Turkey pot pie. Christmas turkey. Pa and Ma and Laura and Mary, sitting around the table for Christmas dinner, with all the fixings. Who else was there? Funny old man with a beard. Mr. Edwards! That was his name. Who was the best friend of the Ingalls family on Little House on the Prairie? Mr. Edwards, of course. That pink triangle is mine. Take that, Mom! Long stretch here. Not much further now. Another thing about these apartments, there's no privacy. Anybody can look into your living room. People are always walking by, staring. I hate it here. See, that family is watching Wheel of Fortune. They look cozy. When I get home I'm gonna shut the blinds. If only we lived on a prairie. I could get along with Laura and Mary. Their Ma is always so nice. Always baking a pie. I wish she was my Ma. I wish Laura and Mary were my sisters, instead of Rachel. Almost there. Last turn. When I get back, first go to the bathroom, then beat Mom at the game. Just have to make sure we're done before The Wizard of Oz. I can't believe I used to think the tornado was a brontosaurus. What an idiot. The flying monkeys are kind of cool. Kind of scary. Not really, but a little. Are those real? Definitely not. I bet Mom will tell Rachel to cover her eyes. She'll be scared out of her wits. Hilarious. It's really strange that nobody else is outside. It feels like a ghost town. Too cold. Quiet. Finally here.

MAIL WALK

Come on, get the right key. Which way does it go? Never get it right the first try. Maybe this time will be different. Damn. Okay, here we go. Junk mail. Figures.

The mailboxes stood at the center of the apartment complex and was the best vantage point from which to observe the layout of everything. Behind me were the older apartments, two-story buildings with wooden siding and barn-style roofs. In front of me was the maze of newer apartments, where we lived, white-plastered hives crammed together.

A dirt walkway went down a slope from the mailboxes and connected with a darkened community center. The pool outside was tarped for winter and the gate was padlocked. It had been that way ever since we moved in.

I headed home. A wind blew at my back and scuttled dry leaves across my path. As I walked past the same cars and buildings, I couldn't help but notice that everything seemed different in the fading daylight. It had gotten colder. I folded my arms and quickened my pace home. Not long after that, I rounded a corner and recognized our building.

Approaching the front window, I peered inside. I wanted to spy on my mother and sister, thinking I might pound on the glass to give them a scare. To my surprise, the living room was completely dark. The apartment was empty.

1986

I cupped my hands to the glass in order to get a better look.

There was no furniture. No pictures on the walls. The game of Trivial Pursuit was no longer spread out on the floor in front of the television. There was no television. No red bowl of popcorn. No plants on the windowsill. No toybox in the corner. Nothing.

Not only that. My family was gone, too. My mother and my sister. As if they had never existed at all. In that moment, if I had looked down at my own body and saw that it too had vanished, I would not have been surprised. If it turned out I was a ghost, a memory wandering the Earth, that would have at least made some kind of sense.

I walked to the front door and turned the knob, half expecting it to be locked, but it wasn't. The door swung open all the way to the jamb. I entered with trepidation.

All the windows, besides the front, were covered over with newspaper, admitting no light from the outside. It was so dark that if I wasn't already familiar with the layout, I doubt I would have been able to find my way around. My eyes slowly became accustomed to the dimness.

On the floor in the dining room was a plastic tarp, upon which sat two five-gallon buckets, a few dried-out paint rollers, and some used paint trays. There was masking tape around the window frames and the farthest wall was only half painted, as if a renovation had been started but abandoned before completion.

Memories flooded in.

Of my sister running down the hallway waving her favorite storybook at me, a diaper hanging off her butt. Of my mother sitting at the piano, fingers moving gently over the keys, singing to us in a voice I found angelic. Of me jumping on my bed, kicking out my legs, and falling backwards onto a pile of pillows. Of all of us sitting on the back porch one late summer evening, listening to katydids and watching the stars come out one by one.

I moved through the kitchen. The refrigerator was empty. The pantry shelves too. And cabinets. All I found was a random screw, a few coins, and a pair of corroded AA batteries. Nothing else. At the other end was a bifold door leading to the main hallway.

I opened the door and stepped onto bare concrete. The carpet had been ripped up and stacked in haphazard piles. On the ceiling, a smoke detector dangled by two red wires.

There was a stench. I could smell it down the hallway. Sour and decayed. It was so rotten I nearly bolted for the door. But where else could I go? This was my home.

Reluctantly, I continued down the hallway. It was almost completely dark. The doors to the bedrooms were shut. All but one, that is. The door at the very end of the hallway. At one time it had been my mother's room. It was cracked open.

There was a flickering of light coming from inside. As I approached the doorway, I peered in. The light was coming from a candle, melted over a cinder block in the corner of the room. Next to the cinder block was a dingy mattress. And next to the mattress was a dirty saucer, on top of which sat a rusty spoon and piles of burned matchsticks. Beside the plate were opened tin of Vienna sausages, spoiled, and crawling with roaches.

I nearly retched.

Then I saw it. Underneath a blanket on the mattress. The shape of a person. It rolled over and I could see the arm exposed, ashen and covered in scabs. There was coughing, and a raspy, weakened voice cried out. "Don't leave me."

The shape rose from the bed. It was only then I could see its face, illuminated by candlelight. Wrinkled and festering. Two black holes where the eyes should have been. Naked under the blanket it was wearing like a shroud. It rocked slowly back and forth, so frail that it was unable to rise without momentum. As it struggled, I heard whimpering and an unnatural, mucousy growl. Suddenly, it was standing. Towering over me. It had a skeletal chest and a protruded belly, the skin all covered with scar tissue.

A hand reached towards me.

I scrambled out the doorway. In my hurry, I dropped the mail I was carrying and slipped on a grocery store advertisement. By the time I got back to my feet, the shape was upon me, grasping at my shirt. I fought to get free, but it had me now, pulling me closer. There was breath on my neck, like rotten fish guts, and a whisper in my ear, full of torment.

"Ain't got a soul!"

I somehow managed to break away. I made it down the hallway, ran through the living room, and bolted out the front door. I didn't look back, sprinting as fast as I could to a liminal area between two apartment buildings, a grassy dell with trees and a playground. It was a place I knew, and therefore felt safe for the time being.

Resting under the monkey bars, I eventually caught my breath. The playground was still and lifeless, like how I imagine a playground would look on the surface of Mars. It was difficult to reorient myself. Everything was alien.

Then, in the distance, I spotted the Christmas lights on the back deck of our apartment. The ones I was supposed to have taken down weeks ago but hadn't yet.

I took off in that direction.

Once again standing outside the front window, I peered inside. Expecting the worst. But my mother was there, sitting on the couch. She was reading a book to Rachel, who sat on her lap and was eating popcorn from the red bowl on the coffee table. They were both laughing. The game of Trivial Pursuit was spread on the floor, as it had been before I went to check the mail. All our furniture was there. The television, the plants on the windowsill, the piano in the dining room. Everything was exactly as it had been. Except for me.

I was far away. Apart from that world. Home was a place unreachable to me. The life I had known before. My family. They were a million miles from where I stood, outside the window of our apartment, in the twilight of a frigid, January evening. It was a life I could observe from afar, but never take part in. Never again.

But then, Rachel noticed me standing there. Her eyes grew and she jammed a finger in the direction of the window, and mouthed my name with a goofy grin. She climbed down from my mother's lap and ran towards me.

Her face was positively beaming.

CLUBHOUSE

After school, I rode the bus home. My friend Luke and I were not sitting together as we normally did. He was sitting in the seat ahead of mine, next to a pretty girl in the sixth grade. They were chatting, so I waited for a good moment to lean over and ask if he wanted to walk to the gas station later to buy some Garbage Pail Kids cards. Series three had just come out, and we both collected them.

"Can't today," he said. "Kai Palmer wants me to meet him at the hollow stump at four. Maybe tomorrow."

"Oh, okay."

The school bus pulled into the cul-de-sac at the entrance of our apartment complex. The driver pulled on the handle and the door swung open. A dozen kids crowded out and ran down the hill to our respective buildings. Shoelaces untied, backpacks jostling.

As usual, I went straight to the babysitter's. She was a nice old woman with cropped hair who always seemed to be wearing house dresses. Miss Poelke was her name, but

1986

Rachel pronounced it Pee-kee, which I thought hilarious, so I called her that too whenever she wasn't within earshot.

At the babysitter's, I ate a snack and then rushed to complete my homework. By the time I was finished, it was nearly four. I stuffed the workbook inside my backpack and told Miss Poelke I was going outside to play.

"Okay then," she said. "Be careful, sweetie."

The woods behind the apartment complex were deep and wide. My friends and I had spent many afternoons exploring them. The most interesting thing we had ever discovered up to that point was the remnants of an old house. Its foundation was overgrown with kudzu and vines. Digging there unearthed forgotten baby toys, a broken swing set, and a bib with Pooh Bear eating honey, caked in mold and grime. On the far side of the woods was Interstate 20. We had never ventured that far, but the steady whirr of traffic always reminded us it was there.

As I approached the hollow stump, I saw Luke and Kai Palmer. They were lobbing pinecones into a deadfall, as if they were hand grenades.

Kai noticed me and tapped Luke on the shoulder.

"Check it out," Kai said. "Your shadow's here."

Luke turned around. When he saw me, his grin faded. Then he rolled his eyes almost imperceptibly. My insides turned to ice and my face flushed hot. But I tried to play it off.

"Ha-ha. Very funny."

Luke turned to Kai.

"Is it okay if he tags along?"

Kai sized me up, blowing away a strand of hair from his left eye.

"I dunno, man," he said. "He kind of looks like a prep to me."

"I ain't no prep," I defended myself.

Kai wasn't convinced.

"Well, you dress like one," he said, and then shrugged. "Look dude, you gonna tell anybody? This place is a secret. For real."

"Hell no!"

Kai led us through the woods. We stomped over leaves and brush, through brambles and briar patches, until we reached a wire fence with a tree fallen across it. One by one, we climbed onto the trunk and crossed to the other side, balancing with our arms outstretched.

Soon, we arrived at a ridge which overlooked the interstate, about a quarter mile away. On the other side was a steep downward slope, dense with miniature pine trees.

"These are the pine packs," Kai informed us.

He crouched at the edge of the pines and duck-walked into them. Luke and I followed close behind. A minute later we emerged into an open area. Here the ground was flat and covered with a blanket of pine needles. We stood up and had a look around.

There was an old mattress with springs exposed, beer cans and cigarette butts, a stack of adult magazines in a garbage bag, and a fire pit filled with ash. An incredible discovery, to say the least.

Kai told us he found out about it while eavesdropping on some high school kids.

"They were saying Brian Rose brought Diane Bishop out to the pine packs near the interstate. Apparently, they screwed, and he peed in her. Then she got mad and broke up with him."

"Gross, man!"

"That is nasty."

Kai seemed proud of the story.

"I know, right?" He continued. "So, yesterday after school, I came out here and explored the woods until I found it. Pretty cool, huh?"

It was cool, we both agreed.

For the next hour, we sat around the fire pit and daydreamed about the spot's potential as a secret clubhouse, each of us throwing out ideas.

"Only kids who know the answer to a riddle can enter."

"But how will they know the answer?"

"They'll be given the secret after the rite of initiation."

"What rite of initiation?"

A pause.

"We need a rite of initiation."

"Good idea."

"Maybe each person has to bring something of value."

"Bring it to the fire pit, like an offering."

"And getting here won't be easy."

"We need to set up death traps all around the perimeter."

"Hell yeah."

"What if we tied wooden stakes to the branches?"

"And then pin the branches back with a tripwire. That way, if you trip over it, you get stabbed in the heart."

"Just like Rambo!"

"What about a hidden pit?"

"With wooden stakes at the bottom."

"Totally."

"We're gonna need a lot of wood for this."

"Let's go collect some branches."

Luke and Kai stomped off into the woods, leaving me behind.

Under the mattress, I discovered a Ziplock bag containing a few matchboxes. I pulled out a match and lit it, watching the flame burn down to my fingers. My mind was dizzy with the possibilities. I lost track of time experimenting with burning all sorts of things. At some point, I looked up and noticed it had become late.

Kai and Luke had never returned. I figured they must have gone home by then. I put the matchbox into the plastic baggie, and stuffed it back under the mattress, where I had found it. Then, on hands and knees, I crawled out of the pine packs, and made my way home in the fading gloom of the evening.

The next day after school, I returned to the clubhouse. Luke had not been on the bus that afternoon, but I was sure he and Kai would be there.

1986

I topped the ridge and paused to listen. It was quiet, except for the distant whirr of interstate traffic. Every so often a wind blew through the pine trees overhead.

As I descended, someone dropped onto me from above, face painted with mud, brandishing a tree branch. I slipped on the dirt and fell backwards. The person stood over me, blocking out the sun. It was Luke, but not my friend Luke. This Luke looked at me as if I were a complete stranger.

"Who's the greatest ninja in the world?"

"What?" I said, confused.

There was a glimmer of recognition in his eyes. For a moment, my friend returned. But then, he raised the branch over his head, and barked out the same question.

"I said, who's the greatest ninja in the world?"

I got annoyed after that.

"Man, I don't know." I gave it some thought, to humor him. "Snake eyes?"

Luke seemed confused. He dropped the branch and looked towards the pine packs.

"He said Snake Eyes."

Kai's muffled voice sounded from the trees. "Who is that?"

Luke explained. "That black ninja from G.I. Joe."

There was silence as Kai considered it, but then he answered, "Has to be a real-life ninja."

I shrugged, still lying on the ground. "I don't know a real ninja."

Luke rolled his eyes and leaned over me. He whispered, "Sho Kosugi. Say it loud enough for Kai to hear you."

"Sho Kosugi!"
Luke shot out a hand and jerked me to my feet.
I had passed the rite of initiation.

Later on, Luke and I sat around the fire pit whittling stakes. A pile of wood shavings had collected at our feet. Kai was off digging the pit. For some reason, Luke seemed annoyed. He was repeatedly striking his knife against the stick, as if punishing it. We hadn't spoken for several minutes, and it was getting awkward. To fill the silence, I began to chatter.

"Oh man," I said. "Guess what card Michael got in a trade this morning?"

"What?"

"Dead Ted."

"That's cool."

I stopped whittling and allowed the silence to return. At last, I could take it no longer.

"Are you mad at me?"

After my question, Luke really started attacking the stick with his pocketknife, hacking at it with the blade until he dropped both stick and knife on the ground, and then he glared at me.

"What are you talking about?"

"I don't know. You seem mad is all."

"Well, I ain't mad."

"Okay, man. Just asking."

His face flushed red. "I ain't mad. It's just. Nevermind."

"What?"

"It's just with Kai, we can talk about cool stuff. We talk about ninja movies, girls, whatever. Not just kid stuff, like G.I. Joe and Garbage Pail Kids."

He glared into the trees, while I stared at the ground.

"My mom won't let me watch ninja movies," I said, finally.

Luke exploded. "See, that's what I'm talking about. Like, I don't know, dude. Why do you have to make such a big deal out of everything? You're like a frickin' girl!"

He grabbed the stick out of my hand and broke it over his knee, tossing the halves on the ground before marching off into the woods.

I sat there motionless, my heart pounding. I picked up another stick from the pile and began whittling, but lost interest and stopped. A few minutes later, I overheard Kai and Luke. They were laughing about something.

The Ziplock bag was still underneath the mattress. I guess nobody else had discovered it yet, because the matchboxes were still there. I pulled them out.

First, I tore pieces of foam from the exposed area of the mattress where the springs had torn through. Then, I tossed the foam into the fire pit, along with a few pages ripped from the adult magazines. Finally, I struck a match and placed it underneath the makeshift kindling, shielding the flame with my other hand.

It didn't take long before the fire pit was engulfed in

flames. Then the wind caught the smoke and blew it right in my face. I coughed and scuttled upwind.

Kai and Luke reappeared out of the woods, slack jawed. Especially Luke. They came over and stood beside me, watching the fire.

"Holy shit!" Luke said, placing his hand on my shoulder. "How'd you do that?"

Without a word, I pulled a matchbox from my pocket, as if I had them on me the entire time. Luke asked if he could see it, and I handed it to him.

"Keep that one. I have more."

He turned the box over in his hand, rubbing his thumb over the striker.

"Thanks, man!"

"Wanna burn something?" I asked.

Luke grinned and knelt beside me.

I ripped one of the magazines in half and handed him one part, then together we shredded the pages into strips and placed them on the fire pit.

Kai watched on, annoyed.

"Hey, guys," he said, "don't you think we oughta finish digging the pit? We don't have enough stakes either."

But neither of us responded to him. The primal urge to start a fire was too great.

Just before I lit the match, Kai reached out to stop me.

"Come on man, this is dumb. We shouldn't be messing with fire in the woods. It's dangerous. Let's go back to building the death traps."

1986

That gave me an idea.

"I know. What if we made a weapon out of fire? Like a flamethrower."

Kai scoffed. "Bullshit. You don't know how to make a flamethrower."

"Yes I do. My uncle showed me how to make one last summer. It's simple."

That had never happened, but I did overhear my uncle telling my grandfather all about it last summer at our July 4th cookout. So it wasn't a total lie. I repeated what I remembered.

"All you need is a spray can of flammable liquid. One that squirts is best. Like WD-40. Then you set the stream on fire with a lighter or match. Instant flamethrower!"

"Damn," Luke said. "We should make one for the clubhouse. Keep it here. Then whenever a bully comes around, wwwsssshhhhh. Burnt to a crisp."

Kai thought about it.

"I know we have a can of WD-40 at home," he said. "If I bring it tomorrow, can you show us how to do it?"

"Totally," I said.

The rest of the afternoon we spent burning anything that would burn. Magazines, mattress foam, twigs, leaves. Kai went into the woods and brought back a mound of underbrush. He dropped the whole thing onto the fire pit. Luke struck a match at the edge. It was engulfed within seconds. The flames spread and the straw crackled and curled into cinder.

The brush made a lot of smoke. So much that it became impossible to breathe. I told everyone to move upwind, but it was pointless because the smoke was everywhere. We coughed. My eyes stung. Then I panicked and scrambled out of the pine packs, low to the ground where the smoke was less dense. Kai and Luke were behind me.

Upon reaching open air, we collapsed on the ground, still coughing up smoke. Once we were sure everything was going to be okay, we all laughed about it.

The next morning, on the drive to school, my mother caught me off guard. She asked if I could stay with Rachel at the babysitter's that afternoon. Miss Poelke had broken her ankle the day before, while carrying groceries, and needed my help.

That was just my luck. The timing could not have been worse.

"But Mom, I'm supposed to play with my friends after school."

"It's just for today honey, until I can make other arrangements. Your friends will be there tomorrow, I promise."

When we pulled into the school drop-off, I flung the door open and slammed it behind me, without even saying goodbye.

Later that afternoon, at the babysitter's, I slumped on the floor with Rachel and helped her build a fortress out of wooden blocks. Miss Poelke was sitting on the couch, her broken foot propped on the ottoman. She was watching game shows and eating sunflower seeds. At some point, asked me to fetch her a Diet Coke from the refrigerator, which I did of course. God was it boring there. It was the last place on Earth I wanted to be. I kept imagining Luke and Kai at the clubhouse, having fun without me.

My mother was late. It was past seven already. She hadn't even called, which was strange. Me, Rachel, and Miss Poelke were sitting on the couch watching Hawaii Five-O, when a knock came at the door. It was her.

Right away I could tell something was wrong. She set her purse on the kitchen table and came over to give me a hug. Then she asked Miss Poelke to turn on the local news.

On the television was helicopter footage of an enormous fire next to the interstate. Three fire trucks lined the shoulder, blasting streams of water from cannons atop the rigs. At the bottom of the screen was a banner. Uncontrolled Blaze on I-20. A reporter came on the screen, but my mother started to explain. Miss Poelke muted the volume.

"Sorry I'm late," she began, her voice unsteady. "I've been with Bonnie this whole time. It seems this afternoon Luke and another boy were playing with fire in the woods, and it got out of control."

"My goodness!" said Miss Poelke, clasping a hand over her mouth. "Are they okay?"

I said nothing and stared at the carpet.

"Luke is okay. He just breathed in a lot of smoke is all. But they are giving him oxygen. The other boy was holding an aerosol can that exploded in his hand. An ambulance took him to the hospital. He may lose an eye. They weren't sure yet."

"That poor child."

My mother turned to me.

"At first Bonnie thought it was you they brought to the hospital, so she called me at work in a panic. I told her you were here with your sister, but then I thought I should check. In my hurry, I forgot my purse at the office, where I keep my book of numbers, and then I couldn't find you in the phone book, so I couldn't call —"

She was on the verge of tears. Miss Poelke could see that and consoled her.

"Sweetie, it's alright. I would have forgot too in the moment. That sure is scary."

"Thank you," my mother said. "When I left, the fire marshal had arrived and was giving Luke a talking to. Poor kid was still wearing an oxygen mask. There were tears streaming down his face. He was shaken up."

Miss Poelke nodded.

"Well, it'll be a tough lesson for him, but if that other boy loses an eye it'll live on his conscience forever. It is what it is."

My mother noticed I was upset. She asked me to walk Rachel to the car and strap her into the carseat. I gathered

1986

our belongings, and led us out the front door, waving goodbye to Miss Poelke. Rachel was barely awake, stumbling over the welcome mat. I took her hand, and we headed downstairs.

I opened the rear passenger door and helped her into the car seat.

At the far end of the apartment complex, I could see red and blue flashing lights against the buildings. Near the dumpsters, a fire truck and police car were parked catty-corner. A small crowd of people had gathered at the edge of the woods, where trails of smoke and ash emanated from the trees and rose into the evening sky.

As I strapped her in, Rachel pointed at the lights and squealed with delight.

"Christmas lights, Bubba. Look!"

I grumbled under my breath.

"Those aren't Christmas lights, idiot. It's not even Christmas."

My anger got the best of me, and I yanked the buckle of the car seat a little too hard.

"Ouch!"

I felt bad and loosened the strap. She looked at me, confused and concerned.

"What's the matter, Bubba?"

"Nothing," I said.

Once she was buckled in, I slammed the car door and stomped to the other side. I got in and heaved my book bag to the floorboard. I stared out the window, away from the pandemonium at the other end of the complex, into an empty parking lot near the main office.

I had never been so jealous.

DRAINAGE PIPE

Luke picked up a rock and hurled it at the tire swing of the big tree, aiming at the center. The rock arced gracefully through the air, bounced off the tire wall, and thudded onto a worn patch of dirt below the swing.

"Son of a bitch," he said.

Just as I was about to give him a hard time about missing, someone shouted.

"Hey, queers!"

We turned around.

Some luck. It was Jesse Black and his gang, hidden under the shade of a second-floor balcony. They were smoking cigarettes and listening to AC/DC on a boombox.

We usually avoided coming down this way, because we knew it was their hangout spot on Saturdays. But that day we had decided to take a shortcut, stupidly.

"Let's just go," Luke said under his breath.

I nodded, and we began walking towards the opposite hill, ignoring the nasty taunts they hurled our way.

1986

Before we got very far, a clod of dirt exploded against the back of Luke's shirt. There were snickers. Luke stopped, so I did too. Then he began walking again, not wanting any trouble. Which was fine by me.

The next thing I knew, Luke went flailing to the ground. Shoved from behind. Three of the gang encircled us. Jesse walked up and hovered over my friend like a vulture.

"Motherfucker," he said, "when I say hey, you better answer!"

Luke braced an arm in defense.

"Okay, man! Just let us go."

Jesse reared back and kicked Luke hard in the side. He writhed on the ground, grasping at his kidneys. But then, he got up and faced them, curling his fists and biting his lip.

"What's the matter?" Jesse asked, seemingly concerned. "Why you scared?"

Luke shrugged. "I ain't scared."

Jesse sized him up. He nodded at the chain hanging from Luke's jeans pocket.

"What's that chain for?"

Luke glanced down. "What do you mean? It's just a chain."

"What I mean is, what's on the other end of that chain? That's what I mean."

The gang laughed. Luke's face darkened.

"Take it out," Jesse demanded. "I wanna have a look."

At that moment, a car drove by.

We all froze, watching until it vanished around the corner. During that sliver of time, the dark cloud which seemed to be hanging over the scene passed, and we became just a bunch of kids goofing off. The confrontation, the bullying, the threat of violence. It was all play-pretend. None of it was real.

But as soon as the car was gone, the dark cloud returned.

"Take it out, I said."

My friend seemed lost. His eyes darted from person to person, looking for an ally, until he saw me standing in the back. His expression was fearful, yet expectant, as if he wanted me to help. But what could I do?

Accepting defeat, Luke pulled the wallet from his pocket and held it out.

I recognized the leather wallet his father had given him on his last birthday. Embossed on the front was a Chevrolet logo. He loved that wallet as much as he loved his father. It was their shared dream to save up for a 1969 Camaro and restore it together.

Jesse scoffed. "Dude. Where did you get this lame-ass thing? Ford makes the best cars. Chevy sucks ass!"

"My dad gave it to me."

"Then your dad sucks ass too."

Luke grimaced. He shot back, "At least my daddy ain't in prison!"

There was a collective gasp.

Jesse glared, and his face turned red.

"What'd you say?"

1986

Luke was steadfast.

Jesse reared back and slugged him right in the gut.

Luke doubled over and clutched his stomach, letting out a nauseous groan.

The wallet fell from his hand and dangled by the chain at his side.

The gang shouted. "Fuck him up, Jesse!"

"Can't let him talk about your daddy like that!"

"Make his ass crawl through that drainpipe. That'll teach him."

Wicked laughter and murmurs of approval.

Jesse furrowed his brow, and then walked behind Luke and kicked him again. Luke tumbled forward, tripping over the concrete wall surrounding the drain. Once more he regained his footing and faced them.

"No way. I ain't going in there."

The gang slowly surrounded him, as if to prevent his escape.

"Okay. You got two choices," Jesse said. "Tell me your daddy is a queer or go in that pipe."

"My daddy ain't no queer!"

"Then I guess you're going in that pipe."

It seemed to dawn on Luke that Jesse was serious. When it did, he shoved his way through the circle of bullies, wildly thrashing his arms.

Two of them grabbed Luke by the arms and wrestled him to the ground. Jesse got in there and elbowed him on the head. Luke managed to kick one of the boys in the

DRAINAGE PIPE

shin, but another grabbed the wallet chain and jerked on it like he was starting a lawn mower.

The links flew through the air and clanked on the concrete runoff of the pipe.

Jesse picked up the wallet. He smacked it against his hand, smiling.

"You want this back? You gotta crawl through that pipe."

Luke sat on the ground, defeated. His face was reddened. On the verge of tears. His eyes darted around and landed on me, still in the back, as I had been the whole time. His gaze seemed to be asking, why aren't you helping me?

I had no answer for that. Or rather, I had an answer, but it was one I didn't want to admit to myself.

Luke rose to his feet and approached the pipe.

Everyone stepped back to let him through.

At that moment, Luke burst into a sprint.

One boy clawed at his shirt as he passed, but he broke free like a football player. The only mistake he made was to look back to see if anybody was following him. Because of that, he didn't notice the tire swing ahead. It was directly in his path. He smacked into it.

For a brief second, it looked as if Luke was dancing with the tire, his arms embracing it, both of them spinning together. But then he bounced off and fell to the ground.

Dazed and nose bloodied, Luke looked back at us, humiliated.

He scrambled to his feet and took off again, a bit wobbly this time, but soon made it up the opposite hill, and vanished into a building entryway.

Everyone laughed. So did I, to my shame. It was so unexpected that it was hard not to laugh, even though he was my friend.

The tire was still spinning from the collision. A fat, ginger kid walked over and stopped it. He cupped his mouth, shouting at the top of his lungs.

"Run home, you big pussy!"

That snapped me out of it. These were not my friends, and now I was alone.

Taking advantage of the commotion, I headed towards my own apartment building. Seconds later, a voice called out.

"Hey, boy."

What I should have done is what my friend Luke did. Run like hell. But I didn't. Instead, I waved back at them, like a smart ass.

"Hey," I answered back, innocently.

I had almost reached the stairs when my face slammed into the ground.

A knee jammed into the small of my back. Someone grabbed my arm and pinned it behind me, nearly to the breaking point. Stars appeared in the corners of my vision.

"Think you're smart, trying to walk away?"

I sputtered an answer, barely able to breathe. "I just wanna go home."

DRAINAGE PIPE

From afar, I heard laughter. Jesse.

"Tell him if he crawls through that pipe he can go home."

More laughter.

They let me up. I dusted off my clothes, trying not to cry.

Jesse walked up and hooked his arm around my neck. He dragged me to the pipe and shoved me down. The rest of them surrounded me.

The pipe was made from corrugated aluminum. It was about two and a half feet in diameter. A trickle of muddy water was running out. Where the runoff was wet, a thin layer of algae had grown.

Peering inside, all I could see was darkness. Then, from the darkness itself, I heard echoes. Across the road, a few of the kids had crowded around the other end of the pipe, where it emptied into a large ditch. They were laughing and taking turns barking into it, like wild dogs.

Making myself as small as possible, I entered the pipe.

The metal was cool to the touch. It was damp inside and smelled of moldy leaves. Any movement I made seemed to reverberate through the cylinder. Every part of me wanted to back out and run home. But it was too late for that.

Because I couldn't see anything in front of me, I kept waving one hand in front, in case there was anything in my path. Now and then, I could hear the kids on the other side, taunting me. Oddly enough, I found their voices comforting. It made me feel less alone.

1986

I crooked my neck and glanced behind me. It was utterly dark back there. How far had I crawled? And more importantly, how much further was it? Ahead was the same, an impenetrable black.

Then, I noticed a pinpoint of light. The merest glint. At first, I thought my eyes must be playing tricks on me, but no. It was really there. This encouraged me, so I quickened my pace. The glint soon evolved into a disc of light. I thought I must be nearing the end. But something was not right. I had not gone far enough. It was too soon.

I emerged from the pipe into a tiny area. The light I had seen was coming from a storm drain near the top. On the floor of the area was a puddle of water, filled with garbage.

I reached through the storm drain and waved my hand.

"Hey!" I yelled. "Over here."

Several of them crowded around the drain. They were making fun of me. One boy stuck his face inside the opening.

"What'd you stop for?"

I protested.

"This is as far as I can go," I said. "I'm turning around."

"No way, dude."

Another face appeared. The fat ginger.

"Got bit by any snakes yet?"

I didn't answer, so he gave me the finger and disappeared.

I steeled my courage and crawled into the final stretch of pipe.

It will be over soon. Don't think about snakes, or any-

thing else that might be lurking in the darkness. Just close your eyes.

So I closed them, because it made no difference.

Nothing entered my mind. I simply placed my elbows and knees in front of the other. Back and forth. Inches at a time. Then, just as I was making progress, I opened my eyes. In front of me were two orbs, glimmering. Reptilian-like eyes. Maybe ten feet ahead.

I froze.

There's no alligator. It must be something else. There's no such thing inside of drainage pipes at apartment complexes in the city. That would be impossible. Don't be afraid. Move.

Meanwhile, my imagination was going wild, conjuring visions of a vicious maw with fangs, as large as the pipe itself. Waiting to swallow me whole.

But that didn't happen.

I soon realized that what I had mistaken for eyes were in reality slivers of sunlight coming through a pile of leaves and brush. When I reached the obstruction, I dug through it, scooping handfuls behind me. As I did so, the light on the other side grew brighter.

Not long after, I emerged from the final stretch of pipe into an enormous ditch.

I got to my feet. My eyes were not yet accustomed to the daylight, so I squinted into the faces of my bullies. All of them were there. The fat ginger, a boy with an awful case of acne, even a girl was with them. And Jesse Black.

1986

Standing there, having emerged from a prolonged sensory deprivation, I found myself in a dreamy state of mind. I don't know how else to explain it. My surroundings felt unreal. The sunlight. The way things were. It was like everything was made out of clouds and had merely taken on the shape of real things.

I remember Jesse talking. To me. His mouth moved and words came out, but I couldn't understand what he was saying. He stepped forward, getting redder in the face. Angrier. Growling at me. The strained tendons in his neck. The stringy hair dangling over his eyes. The freckles on his face. All those details I could see clearly enough. And I could hear him just fine. Yet everything came out garbled, as if he were speaking a foreign language.

I got the impression that he wanted me to crawl back through the pipe.

Then he was in my face. Eyes fearsome. Finger jabbing into my chest. I saw stars. My vision blurred and darkened at the corners. He had struck me across the jaw. But the thing is, I hadn't flinched. I hadn't tried to duck out of the way. I simply took the blow. Then, before I had completely recovered from the first, another punch landed on my chin. This second was weaker than the first, but still like being hit with a sack of bricks. The third was even weaker. A fourth never came.

I recovered, stumbling and holding my chin. We locked eyes. Then, he glanced away. It was like all the rage had gone out of him. All at once. There was just nothing there anymore, and I finally saw him for what he was. I saw everything for what it was.

The gang broke apart. One at a time they climbed out of the ditch and went their separate ways. They said nothing to each other. There was no more laughing or smirking. Jesse went with them. No ceremony or threats. They just left.

On the ground where we fought, I spotted Luke's wallet, covered in dirt. I picked it up and brushed it off the best I could.

It was getting late. The sun was going down. The crickets in the brush surrounding the ditch were chirping. The cars going by had their headlights on. But I thought I still had time before going home, to return to my friend what had been taken from him.

DOG AND BUTTERFLY

It wasn't the first time I'd seen that dog around the apartment complex, an underfed stray with a wiry, tan coat and squat legs. But something was different that day. It scampered across the playground with terror in its eyes and bellied itself underneath a row of bushes near the maintenance shed, all within a matter of seconds.

At the top of the hill, a small group of three boys and one girl appeared, brandishing sticks. Among them I recognized only two, Jesse Black and Kai Palmer. The former had stopped to catch his breath, smoker that he was. The latter wore an eye patch which covered his left eye.

Rachel noticed me noticing them, and asked what the matter was.

"Nothing," I said, "get down and let's go home."

She was hanging from the monkey bars and kicked her legs at me. In doing so, she lost her grip and landed on the ground.

Crocodile tears welled in her eyes.

1986

"Don't even start," I said, cutting her off. "When mama isn't home, I'm in charge, right?"

She crossed her arms and pouted.

Meanwhile, the kids had descended into the playground area, and were poking into every nook and cranny.

Kai walked over and asked if I had seen a dog.

"No."

He eyed me with suspicion.

"You sure, dude? We saw it run down here."

I merely shrugged. That dog wasn't any of my business.

Kai shook his head, annoyed, and walked off to rejoin the search.

Truthfully, I wanted to get out of there before they decided to pick on us instead of that dog. But my sister wouldn't budge. Out of frustration, I yanked her up by the arm.

She hollered, and I apologized, but insisted we had to go home. So we did, although she was protesting the entire climb up the stairs, asking why we had to go.

"Because I said so," I told her, repeating the words my mother had said countless times before.

She didn't like that one bit, and grabbed my forearm, biting down hard.

"Ouch!"

Then she took off towards the playground.

"You frickin' brat!"

She glanced back, giggling like an imp, but tripped over a clump of grass and tumbled to the ground.

Then came real tears.

"See what you get?"

There was shouting. The girl from the group of kids was crouched near the bushes, calling for the others. They all rushed over. The one boy I didn't know lay on the ground and prodded underneath the bushes with a long stick. A few moments later, the dog scurried past them in a mad dash. But it was too slow. Kai managed to grab it as it went by.

"Got 'em!" he said.

The dog writhed in the arms of its captor but was not strong enough to get free. It nipped and whined in futility. Then it became docile, resigned to its fate.

Kai carried him to the big tree, the one with the tire swing. The others followed.

All this time, I had been watching them, while tending to my sister's hurt knee.

"Kiss it."

"That doesn't even do anything."

"Kiss it," she insisted.

I did, and then suggested we should dress it properly back home. But her attention had turned to the drama unfolding under the tree.

She pointed. "Look, Bubba."

"Yep," I said. "They caught the dog."

"What are they going to do?"

"I don't know, Rachel."

"Are they going to pet him?"

1986

"Maybe."

Jesse went inside the maintenance shed. A few moments later he emerged holding an orange extension cord. Kai took one end of it and tied a loop around the neck of the dog, cinching it tight. The dog yelped, contorting itself to bite the makeshift noose, to no avail.

Next, Jesse unraveled several feet and tossed it over the lowest branch of the tree, on the opposite side from the tire swing. He wrapped the cord around his hand, and stepped backwards a few paces, hesitating momentarily. Then he yanked the cord with all his might.

The dog jerked upwards by the neck and swung in the air like a pendulum. It pawed for the ground in vain. As the cord tightened, it bellowed a desperate, guttural whine that made me feel sick.

I looked at Rachel. Her face was expressionless. She was utterly transfixed, no doubt unable to fully process what she was seeing, yet understanding enough to know it was bad.

It felt wrong for someone her age to witness such a thing.

I picked her up, planning to carry her up the stairs. Then I put her down again. I stood there, confused. I noticed the dandelions in the grass. The wooden beams of the jungle gym. The rows of cars in the parking lot. The buildings around us. The balconies.

On one of the balconies, I saw a Mexican woman smoking a cigarette with her arms propped on the rail.

She had doubtless seen everything that happened. Hadn't said a word.

A thought struck me. Nobody in the world cared about that stray dog. Nobody was going to step in at the last minute. It would hang from that branch until it suffocated to death. Afterwards, they would toss its carcass into a dumpster. Nobody would remember it. And that was how it was going to be.

"Stop!"

It wasn't until I was barreling full speed towards the tree that I realized the voice that had shouted was my own. Then I heard it again, echoing in my ears, from far away.

The next thing I remember, my arm was cradling the dog, unraveling the cord from its neck to ease the tension. When it was loosened enough, I removed it. By that point, I had caught up to myself and became aware of what I was doing.

I glanced around and saw angry faces.

"I oughta beat your fuckin ass!" Jesse said. "That ain't your dog and ain't none of this your goddamn business."

I stood my ground. "Ain't your dog either."

"Hey dude," the other boy chimed in. "We gotta put it down. It's got rabies."

"Stop lying."

The girl lost her patience. "Give it back, you dumb shit! That dog killed a nest of baby squirrels!"

"I don't care what it did!" I shouted back. "You can't kill it."

"Why not?" Kai asked.

But I had no good answer for that. And he knew it.

My sister was watching us from afar. I caught her gaze. The dog was wriggling in my arms. I knew that if I let it go free, they'd just catch it all over again and finish what they'd set out to do. So I held on tight. And then walked away.

As I passed by the kids, they berated me, hurling insults. But they didn't follow, for whatever reason. When I reached Rachel, I told her it was time to go home.

She was amenable. All smiles in fact. Petting the dog, and admiring me from below, as we walked back home.

"My hero!" she said.

At home, we put the dog on the balcony. It poked around, sniffing everything. The wilted plant in the corner, the jeans draped over the railing, the toddler toys strewn on a rug. Finally, it crawled underneath the chair and curled up, tongue wagging at us.

We placed a few slices of bologna and a bowl of water near the chair. It came right over, scarfing down the bologna in two slobbery gulps, which delighted Rachel.

"He loves baloney!"

We took turns petting the dog. I inspected its neck for injury, but there was nothing obvious that I could see. It seemed to be in perfect health. Playful, even.

"What is his name?" Rachel asked.

I shrugged. "Heck, I don't know. We don't even know if it's a boy. Could be a girl dog."

Rachel squatted under the chair, and gently lifted up its tail.

"What are you doing?" I said. "You don't even know what you're looking for."

"Yes I do!"

"What?"

"His thing."

She crooked her neck, and then her eyes lit up.

"Bubba, look!"

I looked. "Well, I guess he is a boy, after all."

She nodded, pleased with her discovery.

"So, what's his name?" she asked again.

"I don't know. What do you think his name should be?"

"No!" she said. "You name him."

I glanced around the patio, hoping for inspiration, but nothing jumped out at me.

"Usually if you can't think of a good name for something, you just call it whatever it does or looks like. What does he look like to you?"

She pondered for a moment, her finger pressed against her mouth.

"A graham cracker!"

I laughed. "No. That's a stupid name for a dog. Why do you say that, because of his fur?"

"What, then?"

1986

"I don't know. Any normal dog name will do. Benji, Harvey, Cujo."

She thought hard for several seconds, and then it came to her.

"Graham Cracker."

After five, our mother arrived home. She entered the front door, sunglasses on, keychain dangling in the lock, carrying a sack of groceries.

"Kids, home!"

Rachel ran inside from the balcony to greet her.

I followed, but stayed a few steps behind, waiting for the right moment. Not that it mattered. My sister blabbed the first chance she got, even though I had told her not to say anything right away.

"We got a dog!"

My mother bustled into the kitchen, setting the groceries on the counter, and began to put things away. A few moments later she finally heard what Rachel had said.

"Did you say dog? What dog?"

My sister pursed her lips and contorted her arms, realizing she had messed up, but unable to recover. Instead, she pointed at the balcony door.

My mother's brow furrowed. She flicked her eyes in my direction, and then headed out to the balcony. I stood in the living room, waiting.

She called out my name. My full name. So I knew I was in for it.

"Absolutely not, young man!" she said. "Where did it come from?"

I told her everything that happened. To the group of kids, to the hanging, everything. My sister stood beside me, not understanding why it had become so serious all of a sudden. Her one contribution to the story was revealing that we had named him Graham Cracker, which only seemed to fluster our mother more.

The dog came out from under the chair, sniffing at my sister's hand.

"Rachel," my mother said, snapping her fingers. "Get away from it. We don't know where it came from or if it's got a disease or anything."

She turned to me.

"Son, do you have any idea what it costs to own a dog? It sure ain't cheap. Who's gonna pay the pet fee every month? Because they don't let you keep pets around here for nothing. Did you even consider that? What about feeding it? Taking it to the vet? And who's going to walk it each day so it doesn't shit all over the apartment?"

I giggled. Couldn't help it. But that was probably the worst thing I could have done.

My mother pointed at the front door.

"Take it outside. Right now. Set it loose in the woods for all I care. Just get rid of it."

What happened next is hard to say. Like earlier, at the

1986

tree, I heard shouting, and only later realized that it was me that was shouting. The words that came out of my mouth didn't sound like me. It was like someone else was speaking. This person was telling my mother that it was important that it was me who had rescued the dog and not some other kid. It meant something. Because if it had been some other kid, maybe the dog would be dead right now, tossed in a dumpster somewhere. But he wasn't dead, because of me, and because it was me, the dog was now my responsibility.

"The Bible says love all creatures, great and small. Isn't that what they taught us? I believed that, Mama. I thought it was true. Please don't ask me to put him outside. They'll catch him again and hang him, and this time it will be my fault!"

Overcome with emotion, I stormed to my room and slammed the door.

I fell onto the bed and cried. It's difficult to say how long I cried. It may have been an hour, but it may also have been a few minutes. But at some point, a knock came at the door, and my mother entered. I saw that she had been crying too. She asked if she could sit beside me. I consented and sat up, making a place for her on the bed.

After a period of silence, I spoke.

"Are you mad at me?"

She exhaled, as if she had been holding her breath, and faced me.

"No, son." she said. "I'm not mad at you. How could I be mad?"

She leaned over and kissed the top of my head. "You're growing up, that's all, and it caught me by surprise. The way you talked."

There was silence. I wanted to apologize but couldn't bring myself to do it.

"I'm going to let you in on a secret about mothers. Even though it doesn't make any sense, a mother secretly wishes her babies would stay babies forever. That way she can always be there to take care of them, and more importantly, she'll always be needed. There's a kind of sadness watching your babies grow up. It goes along with the joy."

After some consideration, I replied, "You're right, mama. That doesn't make any sense."

"What did I tell you!" she said, laughing and brushing away a tear from her eye.

Her laughing set me off, and before long both of us were laughing, probably too hard, but it didn't matter. She told me that if I really wanted to keep Graham Cracker, then he may be happier staying with Nana and Grandpa. They had a dog pen behind their house, which had been empty since Ol' Red passed away. But it would still be my responsibility to take care of him, and spend time with him whenever we visited, because dogs require a lot of love.

I thought that was a great idea and was sure Graham Cracker would be happy there.

We hugged, and then she took me by the shoulders and looked me directly in the eyes.

"I'm very proud of you. What you did today took a lot

of courage. Not everybody has that in them. To stand up for those who are unable to stand up for themselves. That's the kind of person I always hoped you would be. You're growing up so fast, it breaks my heart. One day you won't need me anymore."

But I disagreed, and told her so.

"I'll always need you."

That Saturday, we loaded Graham into the back of the station wagon and drove to my grandparents' house. My grandfather greeted us in the carport, wearing work gloves and a faded bandana around his neck. He had spent the last couple days making the dog pen usable again, clearing the area of brush, repairing holes in the chicken-wire fence, and lining the doghouse with fresh hay. When we set Graham loose in the pen, he zoomed around like he had lost his mind. He was as happy as a dog could be, I reckoned.

After we ate lunch, my mother, sister, and grandmother made a trip to Piggly Wiggly. Me and my grandfather stayed behind to clean up the backyard. While working, I asked him if we could set up the target later and shoot BB guns.

"You got it, kiddo."

We were taking a break in the kitchen when my father called unexpectedly from the road. My mother had told him all about Graham Cracker, but he wanted to hear the story from me.

"Well, son," he said, after I told him everything. "I don't think I've ever been more proud. It's a great thing you did. I'm just so proud to hear all that."

"Thanks, Daddy."

"Maybe when I get back in town, you can introduce me to Ol' Saltine Cracker."

I rolled my eyes.

"Graham Cracker, Dad."

His laughter came through the phone.

"I'm just giving you a hard time. Well, guess I better get back on the road. Love you son. Tell Rachel her daddy loves her very much. I would call back, but I'll be driving all night to make this delivery."

"Love you too."

When I put down the phone, my grandfather was nowhere to be found. I went to the backyard, but he wasn't there either. I approached the dog pen, where Graham was happily digging in the dirt. He noticed me and ran over, jumping at the fence. I unfastened the latch and went inside. Before I could even shut the gate, he was pawing at my legs and slobbering me all over with wet, dog-breath kisses.

"Down, boy!"

There was a vine of honeysuckles growing on the fence post near the doghouse. I plucked a handful of them and pulled the stem and ate the nectar. Then I tossed a few on the ground. Graham sniffed them out and gobbled them up, looking to me for more.

"All gone," I said, holding out an empty palm. "No more."

The doghouse was made to resemble my grandparents' house, painted with the same gray and white trim. It had a front entrance, a window on either side, and even a roof covered with shingles.

I crawled inside and Graham followed me. He circled twice on the hay and lay down, tongue wagging. I leaned against the back wall and stared out the window, slowly petting him. For some time, we listened to the distant noises of the neighborhood.

Even before we got Graham, one of my favorite things to do was to crawl inside the doghouse to be alone. It was such a peaceful spot, with the smell of hay, and the view of the backyard. Sometimes, I would look out the window and daydream a whole afternoon away.

Some time later, my grandfather came out from the basement. He was carrying a cardboard target and a few BB guns under his arm. He dropped everything at the burn pile, and instead of calling me by name, he put two fingers in his mouth and whistled.

I crawled from the doghouse and ran to meet him, latching the pen gate behind me.

We set up the target. He told me to pick out a gun, and show him the safety protocols, which I did. Then we took turns shooting rounds. Whenever I missed, my grandfather reminded me how to brace the gun, aim with just one eye, and maintain a wide stance for stability. As time went by, my shots got more accurate, though I never did hit the bullseye. Eventually I got tired. Consequently, my aim grew sloppy. My grandfather suggested we pack it in for the evening. He told me to collect my gun and the target while he rounded up the other guns.

As I picked up the target, I spotted a butterfly amidst the debris of the burn pile. It was adorned with golden wings and was happily fluttering above it all, aimless as the breeze. Normally, I wouldn't have paid it a second thought, but its brilliance against the ash was striking, like an oil painting come to life.

My grandfather asked me what I was looking at.

"Just this butterfly."

Then, a thought entered my mind. "Hey, grandpa?"

"What's that, now?"

"What will happen if I shoot its wing?"

He thought about it, and then shrugged.

"Only one way to find out."

With that, he headed off towards the basement.

I raised the gun and aimed. As soon as it was in my sight, I pulled the trigger. The metal ball tore through its wing like it was made of paper. The butterfly tumbled to the ground and flitted around in tiny circles. It was covered in ash.

About that time, the others returned from the store. I heard the station wagon pull into the driveway and the car doors open. My mother shouted. "Groceries!"

1986

I dropped the gun and took off to help unload the car.

Proud of myself, I told my mother how I had shot a butterfly through its wing, how it tore like paper, but I could tell she was disappointed.

"I don't know what to say about that, son. What a horrible thing to do."

Instantly, my heart fell.

After dinner, I returned to the backyard.

Everything was now bathed in dusklight. The fireflies had emerged and were flashing intermittently above the lawn. The butterfly was nowhere to be found. I looked everywhere for it, in the ashes of the burn pile, in the surrounding grass, but it was gone.

I heard a familiar whine, and spotted Graham in his pen, dimly visible in the muted light. He was standing on hind legs, front paws against the fence, and gazing at me with those friendly dog eyes, always so full of hope and expectation.

"Good boy," I said.

Then I went inside.

TRUCK STOP

We were headed eastbound on I-70, outside Salina, Kansas, when thunderclouds rose over the horizon and darkened the afternoon sky. Soon the wind picked up. Powerful gusts buffeted against the red Peterbilt my father drove, causing us to veer into the next lane. Torrents of rain began to fall. In the downpour, we could only see a car length ahead. But what had us most concerned was a panicked voice on the CB radio, warning fellow truckers of a tornado that had touched down in the vicinity.

My father sat in the driver's seat. He was gripping the broad steering wheel of the truck, fighting to keep it steady, forearm muscles tensed. I sat in the passenger seat, watching the storm out the windshield. It was like watching a disaster movie, but in real life.

Traffic slowed to a crawl. Vehicles pulled onto the shoulder, emergency lights flashing. We passed a station wagon. In the backseat was a woman breastfeeding. She was smiling down at her baby, who must have been blissfully unaware of the pandemonium. We passed another car. Inside was an elderly woman craning her neck to look at the storm. She looked as if she had seen a UFO.

Our destination was a truck stop at Exit 9. We were already planning to stay there for the night. Fuel up, eat supper, and maybe call home. But it had become a safe harbor for us and other unlucky travelers.

We pulled onto the exit ramp and got in line behind several cars and trucks waiting to secure a parking spot. By the time we found one of our own, it was nightfall. The storm had gotten worse. Rain was blowing sideways, visible in the beam of our headlights.

My father shut down the truck. He tuned the radio to a local weather station. On it there was an emergency broadcast which repeated every few minutes. We learned there was not a tornado in our vicinity, as the trucker on the radio had warned. There were three of them. One F2 and two F1s. They were heading south-southwest, at fifteen miles per hour.

"Is that close to us?"

"I really don't know, son."

We were both hungry, but there was no way we could go outside the truck. Luckily, my father kept a cooler on the floorboard filled with snacks and drinks. That evening, we feasted on Fritos, Sprite, and Nutter Butters. While we ate, the wind howled. It was a haunted sound, low and moaning, unlike anything I had ever heard before. Like a demon from hell.

TRUCK STOP

My father asked if I was scared.

"No."

He looked skeptical.

"You sure about that?"

"I'm sure." I said, my voice unsteady. "Are you?"

"Heck no, I ain't scared. I might be if it was a bear or a mountain lion out there. Something with claws and teeth. But I ain't scared of a few sprinkles of rain. Give me a break."

I laughed.

After the feast, we decided to call it an early night.

I climbed into the sleeper and put on my pajamas. My father filled out the logbook, and then joined me, setting the alarm clock for seven in the morning.

"I sure hope the storm's over by then."

"Me too," my father said. "Goodnight, son."

"Night, Daddy."

"Love you."

"Love you more."

The storm continued through the night. I was unable to fall asleep. My mind was filled with nightmarish scenarios. What if the tornado ripped off the roof, sucking both of us into a whirling vortex? What if the parking lot flooded—

There was a crash. Something metallic. Just outside the truck.

Both of us sat up in the dark. My father switched on

the bunk light. The wind had become so powerful it was rocking the cabin, ever so slightly. I knew it wasn't just my imagination, because the calendar pinned to the curtain went sideways.

More banging.

"What is that?"

"Did you feel the truck move?"

"Yeah."

"I could have sworn it just moved."

"I felt it too."

My father crawled out of the sleeper to take a look. I heard the window being rolled down, and a blast of wind. A few minutes later he crawled back in.

He told me a huge piece of aluminum siding was sitting on the ground next to the trailer. He said the rain was so heavy it was like being underwater. As I tried to sleep, a picture arose in my mind, of our Peterbilt sitting on the ocean floor, surrounded by undulating vines of seaweed and schools of silvery fish.

"Rise and shine, sleepyhead."

It was morning. I opened my eyes and sat up. After putting on my clothes and glasses, I unzipped the curtain and crawled out, squinting in the morning light. But all I could see out the windshield was a wall of grayish mist.

"He's alive!" my father said, feigning surprise. "Bit froggy this morning."

"Yeah, it is."

I moved to the passenger seat and leaned my head against the window, yawning.

My father was studying the road atlas. After several minutes, he rolled it up and stuffed it between the driver's seat and the doghouse.

"Getting hungry?" he asked me.

"Starving."

He laughed. "Well, I guess we better grab some breakfast then."

My eyes lit up. "Do they have pancakes here?"

"Sure do, Kemosabe."

Outside the truck, I breathed in the morning air. It was humid, mixed with a pungent—yet somehow pleasant—aroma of diesel fuel. There were tractor-trailers parked close to ours. In the fog, it was impossible to see how full the parking lot was, but from the clattering of engines, both near and far, there must have been dozens of trucks.

We crossed the parking lot to the main entrance. The only way to tell which direction to go was the faint silhouette of the gas station island. At some point, a man with a long beard emerged from the fog like an apparition and startled us. He was carrying a cup of coffee and a pack of chocolate donuts, nodding politely before vanishing in the other direction.

1986

My father took me by the hand out of caution, but I pulled away.

As we approached the entrance, it became obvious the truck stop had not been spared the wrath of the storm. Out front, a large window was busted out, and tiny shards of glass were scattered all over the ground. Two workers were busy hanging a blue tarp over the empty window frame. Another was sweeping.

"Mind the glass," he said, as we went inside.

The power was out. It was dark, but there was just enough light coming in from the windows for customers to shop. And they were. The clerks were behind the counters, tallying up purchases with pen and paper. The mood inside was unsettling, though I find it hard to say why. I asked my father if we should go back to the truck. He suggested we check out the restaurant first, to see if they were serving breakfast, which was okay by me.

The restaurant in the truck stop was called The Blue Skillet. Apparently, we were not the only ones looking for a hot breakfast that morning. It was absolutely jammed with customers, with a line outside the entryway. Luckily, the line was moving fast, and we were seated fifteen minutes later.

The waitress brought menus. She asked my father if he wanted coffee, which he did. She seemed frazzled, and was even short-tempered with us, which contrasted with the Have a Nice Day button pinned to her apron. It was bright yellow with a smiley face.

"Do you have pancakes?" I asked.

She frowned and shook her head.

"Normally we do, but the griddle is down, sweetie. Poor Reginald back there is the only cook who even bothered to show up this morning."

"Y'all busy," my father observed.

She rolled her eyes. "Hell, it always gets like this after a storm. Folks lose power at their houses, so they go out to eat. Dumbasses don't stop to think we can lose power too."

She hurriedly took our order, and then rushed off to the next table. My father hunched over the table and whispered to me.

"What a B-I-T-C-H."

I laughed.

"Don't tell your mama I said that."

"I won't."

The food arrived and we dug in. My breakfast was scrambled eggs, hickory bacon, and toast with butter. Orange juice to drink. It was the most uncomfortable meal I can remember, sitting in the dim light coming in through the windows. Though the dining room was full, it was eerily quiet, as if everyone was afraid to speak above a whisper. The only sounds were the clanking of silverware and the pouring of drinks into cups.

About halfway through breakfast, the power came back on. People in the dining room cheered. It felt like a different place. The cook behind the counter did a spin and a little dance with his spatula. The jukebox started playing country music. Everything was back to normal.

After paying for the meal, we headed to the payphones. My father needed to check in with the dispatcher about our next pickup. He called and was informed to lay over in Salina for the time being. That was good news. We could use the break.

The first order of business was to shower. The second was laundry.

We walked out to the truck to grab our toiletries and dirty laundry and returned to the showers. The girl behind the counter checked us in and gave us the key to a stall.

We showered, lathering ourselves with soap and shampooing our hair. A powerful jet from the shower head massaged my neck and back, washing away a week's worth of dirt and grime. Standing next to my father, I couldn't help but notice that his was not like mine. His was surrounded by hair, with a mushroom cap on the end.

I was done first. I stepped out and dried off with a fluffy towel. It felt great to put on a clean set of clothes. While I waited for my father, I played with his gold Timex watch, stretching and twisting the metal band around my wrist.

My father began singing in an obnoxious voice. On the Road Again by Willie Nelson. He sounded just like a donkey braying. Getting the words wrong.

"It's like my love is mak-in music with my friends…"

I rolled my eyes.

"Dad!"

"What?"

"That's annoying."

"Aww, you're no fun."

Afterwards, we found the laundromat, down a long hallway near the payphones. The air inside was hot and smelled of detergent. There were dozens of machines. The fluorescent lights were buzzing and flickering. Nobody seemed happy to be there.

An old woman sat in a chair, reading a magazine. She grimaced at us, when we set our laundry down near hers. There was also a man in a tattered suit, standing in front of the coin dispenser. His face was painted white, and he was wearing an orange wig underneath a bowler hat. I briefly made eye contact with him, but he looked away, as if embarrassed. Then, he went to a dryer and pulled the clothes into a laundry basket and walked out.

"Don't see that every day," my father said.

We loaded a machine and emptied a packet of detergent on top. My father let me put the coins into the feed and push to start. Once the laundry was going, there was nothing to do but sit and wait.

We found a spot on a row of chairs against the wall and sat down. Within five minutes of sitting in the heat, listening to the motion of the agitators and the slopping of clothes in soapy water, I nodded off. Then a few moments later I jolted awake. It was beyond boring.

1986

"Daddy," I said.

My father was flipping through a Field and Stream magazine.

"Son."

"Can I go sit in the truck?"

"What for?"

"I'm bored."

"What are you gonna do in the truck? Boring out there too."

"I don't know. Listen to the radio. Look at the road atlas. Anything but this."

He considered it. I could tell he sympathized.

"Not sure I like the idea of you being out there by yourself."

It took some convincing, but he eventually agreed. He made me promise to keep the doors locked, and not to touch anything except the radio. Most importantly, he added, do not leave the truck under any circumstances. I promised all that, so he walked me back to the truck and disappeared back into the fog, leaving me by myself.

The first thing I did was to put on music.

Fishing through the cassette briefcase, I found Willie Nelson's Greatest Hits, and inserted it into the deck. Then I fast-forwarded to On the Road Again. Three playthroughs later, I was convinced the lyrics my father had sung in the shower were nowhere to be found in the actual song. It was no big deal. I had misheard lyrics plenty. But I had never known my father to make a mistake like that. The rest of the album played through while I sat in the passenger seat and stared at the fog.

At some point, I pulled out the road atlas and laid it open on the doghouse. I turned to Kansas and found Salina, tracing my finger southbound along the interstate, and calculated how many miles we were from Georgia.

About that time, my stomach began to bubble, and I had to go. Like, bad.

I didn't know what to do. Should I go inside? But my father had made me promise not to leave the truck. Besides, I wasn't even sure I could make it all the way to the restrooms before—

My insides churned. There was a dull ache in my bowels. It took all my strength not to go in my pants. I quickly found a small paper bag underneath the cooler. I unwadded it and pulled down my pants, standing awkwardly in the footwell. Then, I did my business, hoping nobody could see what I was doing.

It was over. I was relieved.

But then, another problem. What will my father think when he comes back and sees what I did? He'll probably get mad at me. He'll ask why I didn't just go inside and use the restroom, like a normal person. But he might also get mad if I did go inside, after forbidding me to do so. Maybe it will be okay, if I just explain what happened. It wasn't my fault. When you have to go, you have to go. While I debated with myself, the paper bag sat on the doghouse. Shaming me.

1986

I turned off the radio. Then I grabbed the paper bag and climbed down from the truck, leaving the door unlocked for when I returned.

The parking lot felt different without my father there. Bigger and more threatening. It was hard to know which way to go. I looked for the silhouette of the gas station island, but quickly became disoriented. It was like walking in a maze without walls.

Somehow I found the entrance. The ground in front of the door was still littered with tiny shards of glass, though someone had thought to set out a wet floor sign. The broken window was covered with the tarp, sealed haphazardly around the edges with duct tape. I went inside and headed straight to the laundromat.

My father was not there. Nor could I find our laundry. There was a family sitting where my father and I were sitting an hour ago. I thought about asking them if they had seen him but was too timid to do that.

I panicked. My mind was whirling. What should I do? Return to the truck. Yes. Simple. Maybe we had even crossed paths in the fog, without seeing one another. Maybe he was there now, wondering where I had gone.

As I ran out the entrance, I nearly slipped on the shards of glass, but caught myself at the last moment. In doing so, I dropped the paper bag, but quickly picked it up again, and rushed across the parking lot. A couple minutes later I stopped. Something was not right. The walk had not taken so long before. I turned around and could no longer see the truck stop. In every direction there was only a grayish mist.

My heart was pounding. I listened carefully to my surroundings. Nearby, I heard cars driving on the pavement and people talking. I took off in that direction. Then, out of the mist, a Buick emerged. It wasn't going very fast. The driver saw me and slammed the brakes. The car honked, and the driver made a rude gesture out the window. I avoided eye contact and kept walking. Eventually, the silhouette of the gas station island reappeared and I breathed a sigh of relief.

I paced down the aisles of the gas station store, finding it hard to think straight. My eyes darted in every direction, hoping to find my father. At the counter, a man stood in line wearing a work shirt, much like the one my father wore. His back was to me. I walked around to get a better look, and he stared down. It was a stranger. Behind him stood an elderly Black man, carrying a newspaper. He wouldn't get out of my way. That frustrated me. All this wasted time. The entrance door opened and a group of teenagers came inside. They were laughing. The clerk behind the counter looked completely bored, as if this was the last place on Earth he wanted to be. At the other end of the store was an arcade with slot machines and video poker. My father wasn't there either. Why would he be? Next to the arcade was a radio shop with a neon sign over the entrance. Along the aisles were tools and accessories for big trucks, along with a glass display filled with CB radios. Not there.

1986

I returned to the laundromat. Maybe he had only left temporarily—to make a call, or to buy something—and maybe he had taken the laundry with him so it wouldn't get stolen. Maybe. But it was completely empty. There was not a soul anywhere.

Unsure where to go next, I continued down the hallway. It was the one place I hadn't looked. At the end of the hall was a wooden door, and on the door hung an ivory crucifix.

It was a small chapel. The space was dimly lit and smelled like an ashtray. The lights were off, but there was a window covered in stained glass cellophane that was peeling at the edges. Daylight filtered through the window and rainbowed across the floor. In the front of the room, hanging on the wall, was a velvet painting of Jesus, kneeling in prayer.

"How you doing, young man?"

The voice startled me. I had not seen him, sitting in the back.

"It's all right," he reassured me. "Come over here for a second. My ears ain't too good."

I moved to a spot where I could see him better.

He was an older man, about fifty. Bone thin. Wearing a mismatched suit that was too big for him. There were smudges of white paint around his receding hairline. In a duffle bag next to him, was an orange wig and bowler hat. He noticed me looking, and grinned.

"Can you believe that? There was a circus clown in

TRUCK STOP

here, right before you came in. I don't know where he went off to. Left his hat, his wig, and all his worldly possessions!"

The man let out a wheezing laugh. As he laughed, he absently reached into the bag and pulled out a sucker, unwrapping it and sticking it in his mouth. When I didn't say anything, he looked concerned.

"What's the matter, son? Everything okay?"

I told him I couldn't find my father. How I had left the truck, and all the rest of it. As I spoke to him, I realized I was crying and tried to stop.

"Hey, now," he said, patting the seat of the chair next to him. "It's gonna be fine, I promise."

I sat down next to him. It made me feel better just to know I wasn't alone. He proceeded to ask what my father looked like, where I had last seen him, and where all I had looked so far.

As we talked, I couldn't help but stare at the sucker rolling inside his cheek. Not that I wanted one, but it was hard to ignore. He took my staring as a cue and opened the duffle bag. It was filled with candy and tchotchkes made of plastic. He said I could take anything I wanted, so I grabbed a pineapple sucker to be polite.

"Thanks."

"Heck, that's not my candy," he said. "That belongs to Flippity Flop. But I won't say anything if you won't. And you won't, right?"

"No."

"Good man," he said. Then he followed up with a question. "Hey, do you like magic?"

I didn't answer, which seemed to frustrate him.

"Okay then, be that way."

He sat there, and then he nodded as if something had dawned on him.

"Oh, I remember now. You're worried about finding your daddy."

"Yeah."

"Well, I'm sorry. I should have known better. Believe it or not, I know how that is. But here's the thing, son. Even when life ain't going your way, sometimes you gotta look on the sunny side, you know it?"

He pulled a deck of cards from his jacket pocket. On the back of the cards was a moon wearing a dour face, surrounded with silver filigree. He shuffled the deck, fanned the cards, and presented them to me, facedown.

"Pick a card."

I chose one.

"Good man. Now, take a look at the card and insert it back into the deck anywhere you like."

I did as he said. Then he reshuffled, cut the deck a few times, and drew a single card, displaying it between his thumb and fingers. The look on his face said I should have been impressed, but I wasn't.

"That's not my card," I said.

"Oh, no. Really?"

"Yeah."

"That's unfortunate. But wait a minute."

"What?"

"Do you remember what I told you before?"

I shrugged, not comprehending.

"Sometimes," he said, "all you gotta do is look on the sunny side."

He flipped the card over, and instead of the moon face, there was a sun face, surrounded by a golden filigree.

I smiled.

"You see? Things ain't so bad. Could be worse."

"I guess so."

"We'll find your daddy soon. Don't you worry."

"Thanks."

He handed me the card.

"Here, you keep this. Consider it a reminder."

Without a thought, I opened the paper bag and dropped the card inside.

The man stuffed the incomplete deck back into his jacket pocket. There was momentary silence, and then he snapped his fingers.

"I just had a great idea!"

"What?"

"You said your daddy is a truck driver, right?"

"Yeah."

"It just so happens I got a CB radio out in my truck. We could use it to call your daddy."

It made sense to me, if he was listening.

"You know his call sign?"

1986

I did, and told him.

"That's a good one. I like that for a call sign. You know, I bet anything he's out in the truck right now, listening to the CB, trying to find out where the heck you are. And even if he's not, we could ask one of the other truckers to help us find him. What do you think?"

"I don't know."

"Worth a shot, right?"

I agreed, and we left the chapel. We went down the hallway, past the laundromat, and the payphones, and turned the corner, headed to the main entrance. As we passed The Blue Skillet, a woman's voice called out.

"Excuse me, sir?"

I turned and saw the waitress from earlier that morning, the one with the Have a Nice Day button pinned to her apron. She was following us.

The man pressed on my back, hurrying me towards the entrance. He was staring straight ahead, pretending not to hear.

The waitress addressed me.

"Hey, baby," she said, overtaking us. She put out an arm to block the doorway. "Do you know this man?"

All I remember next is the waitress asking the man questions. Who he was, and where he was taking me. He didn't say anything to her, just stared at the floor, muttering to himself and avoiding eye contact. Then, out of nowhere, he shoved the waitress aside and burst through the doors, running straight into the fog. Seconds later, there was a screeching of tires and the blaring of a car horn. A car door opened, and a few moments after that, a woman screamed. The waitress took me by the hand and walked me to The Blue Skillet. She knelt so that we were on the same level.

"Listen, hon," she said. "I want you to go into the restaurant and sit in that booth in the corner. I'll come find you in a little bit. This ain't nothing for a child to see."

I did as she said. It was something in her voice, a seriousness, that made me obey without question. From the booth, I watched everything else unfold.

An elderly man wandered inside. He was wearing shorts, black socks, and a field hat. He seemed bewildered. The waitress approached him and wrapped her arm around his shoulder. He smiled. Then, remembering he was indoors, he removed his hat and ran a frail hand through what was left of his hair. He dropped the hat, and the waitress stooped to pick it up. She guided him to a phone behind the register. Then she made a call with him standing there. Around the same time, an elderly woman came inside. Her makeup was smeared around the eyes. She joined the elderly man, and they hugged. After the waitress hung up the phone, they went back outside. Then, over the next half hour, several truck stop workers ran back and forth, carrying things, and shouting instructions to others inside the store. Soon an ambulance arrived, or what I thought to be an ambulance. There was a siren whine and a red light flashing in the mist.

Eventually, the waitress returned to The Blue Skillet.

Her face was pale and devoid of expression. She noticed me staring at her across the dining room and brightened. After speaking with the cook through the service window, she filled a glass of orange juice and brought it over to me.

"I didn't know what you liked, but I had a guess."

She winked and sat down in the seat across from mine. I drank the orange juice, while she watched on, not speaking for several minutes.

"You know," she said, breaking the silence, "I just had a feeling. About that man. I had seen him around here before, in that clown makeup. And I remembered you from breakfast. You and your daddy. When the power was out."

Her voice trailed off. She looked past me, to somewhere far away. Then, she returned, seeming embarrassed. To change the subject, she pointed at the paper bag sitting next to me.

"What you got in the bag there?"

I said nothing. Then, my eyes welled with tears, and my voice broke.

"Can you help me find my dad?"

The waitress covered her mouth, and gasped.

"Oh, darlin. You're lost. I should have known that. Listen, stay right here and I'll fetch the manager. Don't you worry, honey, we'll find your daddy!"

She left. Five minutes later, an announcement blared over the truck stop intercom, asking for anyone missing a child to come to The Blue Skillet. A few minutes after that, she returned. She told me not to worry, that, believe it or not, this was not the first time a child had been separated from their parents. She then removed the Have a Nice Day button from her apron and gave it to me.

"Take this," she said. "I think you need it more than I do."

I held the button and smiled.

"Thanks."

She glanced outside, where the ambulance lights were still flashing.

I asked her what happened and looked back at me. Her eyes fell, as if searching for the right words.

"The thing is, he fell—"

The cook arrived at the booth, wearing a grimy apron. He set down a plate of pancakes and bacon, with a bottle of maple syrup on the side. He also had a cup of coffee for the waitress, who nodded graciously.

"Thank you, Reginald. Appreciate that."

"Yes, ma'am!" he said, and hopped back to the kitchen.

I drenched the pancakes in syrup and dug in. Meanwhile, the waitress sipped on her coffee and watched me eat.

"What's your name?" I asked, out of curiosity.

"Mary Beth."

Then, something occurred to me.

"Are you a mom?"

She nodded sweetly yes and gazed into the empty dining room. A tear ran down the side of her cheek. I

1986

asked no more questions after that and finished my meal in silence.

Some time later, a police officer came into the dining room and stood by the register. He was carrying a notepad and pencil. When he spotted us, he waved Mary Beth over. She told me to stay put and said she'd be right back.

They talked for a while, him writing in the notepad. Every so often she gestured to me. That made me nervous. They stared while they talked. I started to feel trapped. Something about that police officer. Wearing a uniform and carrying a gun in the holster. It made everything feel more real. Before, everything had felt like a dream, but now I was awake. I was alone in a truck stop, somewhere in Kansas, hundreds of miles from home. Surrounded by strangers.

Without thinking, I opened the paper bag, and placed the Have a Nice Day button inside. Then, when neither the waitress nor the officer was looking my way, I snuck from the booth. I crept behind the counter and pushed my way through the saloon doors to the kitchen. It was the only other way out of the restaurant. If you had asked me what I was thinking at that moment, I wouldn't have been able to tell you. I only knew I had to get away.

The kitchen was small. There was only a single person back there. Reginald, the cook who had brought out my food earlier. He was standing at the sink, washing dishes. He turned when the doors swung open and grinned at me.

"Hey there, little man," he said. "Wanna do some dishes? Pay off them pancakes?"

TRUCK STOP

There was a wooden door at the back of the kitchen, next to a rack of pots and pans. I took my chance and made a break for it. The door opened into a long corridor.

"Boss man, where you goin? It ain't break time yet!"

I made my way down the corridor, hoping to find another door that would lead me outside. The lighting was poor, emanating from exposed light bulbs hanging from wires along the ceiling. The floors were dingy. Along the walls were shelves of restaurant supplies, stacks of boxes, an old soft drink dispenser, and a broken-down fryer, metal hoses protruding from the back. This place was nothing like the rest of the truck stop. Everything smelled like mud. It was as if I had stepped into decades past.

There was a sickness in the pit of my stomach. I was not thinking clearly. If you had told me it would have been smarter to wait inside the restaurant for my father, I'm not sure I would have even understood. Such was my state of mind.

I entered a pantry. Along the walls were shelves stocked with canned goods. On the right was a staircase, decrepit looking, but I noticed a glint of light, so I headed upstairs to have a look around. Not surprisingly, it was another pantry area, larger than the one below. It was filled with sacks of flour, rice, and beans. Dry goods. But the most interesting thing up there was another staircase, leading up to a horizontal door on the ceiling. The doorway was opened, and light from outside bathed the pantry in a somber, muted light. I decided to climb those stairs too.

1986

At the top of them, I found myself standing on the roof of the truck stop.

It was a wide area of concrete, dotted with ventilation fans. To me, they looked like tarnished, aluminum mushrooms. In the middle of the roof sat a gigantic HVAC unit. It made a buzzing drone sound. The floor was scattered with debris from the storm. Next to the doorway was a plastic garbage bag, half-filled with trash. I could see nothing beyond the rooftop except for the wall of fog, as thick and impenetrable as it had been all morning.

Of course, my father was not up there. Nothing was, really. So I turned to head back downstairs. Just as I did, I heard a weak chirping nearby.

I paused to listen closer. It was hurting, whatever it was. Suddenly, it became very important for me to find the source. I wandered the entire roof, using its song as a beacon. Eventually I found it, lying in a little nest on the edge of the rooftop balustrade.

The nestling was tiny, with pinkish skin. It had little beads for eyes, and a beak that was opened wide, chirruping the same song. One of its wings appeared to be broken. The creature was so fragile in appearance, it made me wonder how on Earth it had survived the storm. And yet it had. I lifted it from the nest and held it against my chest. To give it warmth, I suppose. Or solace. I don't know why.

As soon as I picked it up, the singing stopped. Perhaps I could help it somehow, I thought. Take it with me. Feed it worms. Nurse it back to health.

TRUCK STOP

My thoughts drifted to my family. My father and mother. My sister and grandparents. Never had I felt so distant from the people I cared about, those who had protected me, all my life. I was completely alone. But not only me. That was the true reality of everything that was alive or had ever lived. Family was temporary. You will lose them all. In time. Every single person you ever loved, or that ever loved you, will be lost forever. The proof was in my hand.

I recalled my father's terrible singing in the shower. How I made fun of him. I would give anything to hear his voice again. I don't care if he sings the wrong words anymore. It doesn't matter. I then recalled how I pulled away when he tried to hold my hand. How stupid I was. How thoughtless and unkind. Let me take it back. Let me do it over. I will make it right.

The creature stirred in my hand, as if preparing to take flight. I held it aloft, not wanting to hold it back. Wanting to help it however I could. But it collapsed and grew very still, and I knew, even without knowing, that it was dead.

The next moment may be a false memory, or merely what I want to believe, but I'm almost sure it happened. I felt the sun shining on my face. I looked up and sunlight blinded me. I squinted my eyes, and when I opened them again, the fog was dissipating. Every second I could see further across the parking lot. And after a few minutes, I could see clear to the interstate, where cars and trucks were going by. I could see the fields across the road. And

1986

blue sky. And white clouds. I saw the ambulance driving across the parking lot and merging onto the main road. The lights were no longer flashing.

Then I saw my father, wandering through the parking lot, looking frantic and lost.

"Daddy!"

He heard me but couldn't figure out where the voice was coming from. I waved my arms and continued to shout. Then he saw me and waved back. He ran towards the main entrance.

I placed the creature back into its nest and placed the nest inside the paper bag. Then, I went downstairs and retraced my steps down the corridor, through the kitchen, and the dining room, until I reached the entrance lobby.

My father knelt and pulled me into an embrace.

"Oh God. Thank you, God," he said.

His voice was quivering.

"I thought I lost you forever."

He was crying. I had never seen him cry before. He took me by the shoulders and made me promise never to wander off again. Never leave the truck. Never. There were tears in his eyes, and he hugged me again.

I saw Mary Beth standing outside The Blue Skillet. Her hands were clasped to her bosom, as if in prayer. She was smiling, and there were tears in her eyes too.

My father noticed the paper bag I was carrying and asked me what it was.

I handed it over. He opened it and looked inside.

BLIZZARD

To be honest I had my doubts. They had been growing over time. Therefore, I had decided to find out the truth for myself, once and for all. To see with my own eyes what I had only heard from others, up till then. It was the only way to be sure.

Nestled in my bed, under the quilted blanket my grandmother had sewn for me, I merely pretended to be asleep. The door to our bedroom was closed, but even so I could hear the muffled cheer of holiday festivities occurring just down the hall. Laughter, music, glassware clinking. My sister was soundly asleep in her own bed. Outside, a gale howled through the eaves and wisped in through tiny gaps in the window frame. My attention drifted from the storm outside, to my sister, to the adult merriment, and back again.

I opened my eyes. It must have been hours later. The house was utterly silent.

1986

Climbing out of bed, the air was frigid. My breath came out like smoke. I pulled on my long johns, tiptoeing across the wooden floor so not to creak. Once dressed, I approached the bedroom door and carefully turned the knob. As the door opened, a warmth like a fireplace enveloped me.

The hallway was dark. It took some time for my eyes to adjust to the shadows, but soon I recognized familiar shapes. The bookshelf, the toy piano, the framed pictures of dead relatives along the walls. I made my way down. As I passed by my grandparents' room, I thought it was strange that the door was closed. That had never been the case before.

As I entered the living room, a powerful gust of wind blew the front door open. It smashed into a cabinet where my grandfather stored his guns. The noise was so loud, I was sure it would wake up my family. I rushed over to shut the door, but hesitated when I looked outside and saw the winter desolation. Everything in the front yard was blanketed in white, as if they were memories of things I had once known faded by the passage of time. The details seemed to be lost, and only impressions remained. The station wagon. The oak tree. The mailbox. All covered in snow. The wind drove a steady stream of ice and snow, swirling chaotically, obscuring everything that lay beyond the driveway in a pale darkness.

I managed to close the door, and everything was quiet.

Near the front window was a table, and on the table was a small evergreen tree draped with ornaments, silver tinsel, and strands of incandescent lights every color of the rainbow. The tabletop was covered with a white cotton blanket, emulating the reality I had just witnessed outside. And there were gifts wrapped in festive paper and bows, neatly arranged around the base of the tree.

On the floor near the table were yet more gifts, these unwrapped and on display. Toys and board games and winter clothes. Meant for me and my sister. No question about it. I could hardly believe my eyes. Some gifts I had dreamed about, while others were a total surprise.

There was a Lite-Brite, illuminated and decorated with a clown face. The game of Mouse Trap, completely assembled and waiting for someone to trigger its complex mechanism. Hungry Hungry Hippos, with a plethora of white marbles in the center of the board.

Behind those was the whole collection of Masters of the Universe, the action figures assembled around Snake Mountain, with a giant serpent emerging from deep within the castle. He-Man and the heroic warriors of Grayskull battling Skeletor and his evil warriors. Man-At-Arms, Ram Man, Teela, Orko, and Man-E-Faces against Mer-Man, Trap Jaw, Kobra Khan, Tri-Klops, and Two Bad.

But that wasn't all. Because right next to them was a complete set of G.I. Joe: A Real American Hero. Combat Jet Skystriker and Cobra H.I.S.S tank on a battlefield that also included Snake Eyes and Timber, Dusty, Tomax and Xamot, Ripper, Torch, B.A.T.S, Monkeywrench, Xandar, Beach Head, Scarlett, Cobra Commander, Destro, Snow

1986

Job, Blowtorch, Lady Jaye, Flint. Also Zartan, whose skin turned blue in sunlight, and the Swamp Skier. And the one I had wanted most of all, Storm Shadow, the Cobra ninja.

I couldn't believe my eyes when I saw there were Transformers, both Autobots and Decepticons, fighting over the fate of planet Earth. Megatron, Bluestreak, Skywarp, Bumblebee, Rumble, Mirage, Sideswipe, Thundercracker, Ironhide, Jazz, Laserbeak, Brawn, Gears, Optimus Prime, Sunstreaker, Ratchet, Soundwave, Reflector, Cliffjumper, Shockwave, Windcharger, Brawn, Ravage, Starscream, Prowl, Huffer, Trailbreaker, Wheeljack and Hound. Hot Rod, Rodimus Prime, Blaster, Shockwave. Even Omega Supreme.

And the best gift of all, a Nintendo Entertainment System with Light Gun and R.O.B. the Robot. Along with many Game Paks, including Super Mario Bros, Duck Hunt, Commando, The Legend of Zelda, Metroid, Kid Icarus, R.B.I. Baseball, Mega Man, Castlevania, Mike Tyson's Punchout, R.C Pro-Am, and Kung Fu.

Besides all these, there was a football, a baseball glove with three baseballs, a miniature basketball hoop for the bedroom, and a stocking with my name written in glitter, filled to the brim with Hershey's Kisses, caramels, candy canes, an orange, five packs of Garbage Pail Kids cards. Even a roll of quarters.

It was everything I had ever wanted. Could ever hope to want. I was so happy, my mind reeling with the promise of endless hours of fun.

Just as I was about to start playing with my new toys, I happened to notice the dish and glass cup on the end table. Before my sister and I went to bed, we had set out cookies and milk. To my astonishment, the cookies had been eaten, except for a few crumbs here and there, and half the glass of milk had been drunk.

From the kitchen there came a loud crash. I bolted to my feet to see what it was. As I entered the kitchen, a delicious aroma filled the air. It was dark inside, so I switched on the light.

"Hello?"

There was no answer.

The kitchen table was set for a feast. In the center sat an empty Blue Willow serving platter. Next to it was a turkey, stuffed and roasted to a chestnut brown, garnished with herbs, onions, and carrots. Surrounding the main dishes were smaller plates and bowls. There was crockpot macaroni and cheese, homemade mashed potatoes, green bean casserole, sweet potato casserole, cranberry sauce from a can, roasted corn on the cob slathered in melted butter, a tray of deviled eggs, sprinkled with paprika, traditional stuffing with pieces of sausage and diced onion and celery, chilled ambrosia salad made with whipped topping, chunks of banana, slices of mandarin, cherries, all mixed together with chopped pecans, fresh green peas, and a boat of brown gravy.

On the pantry table were all the desserts. A fruit cake, my aunt's famous carrot cake with the creamiest, richest

1986

frosting you ever tasted, a red velvet cake, a chocolate cake with no frosting, two pecan pies with slightly burnt edges and a crispy surface layer of filling, two pumpkin pies, the custard cracked and bulging at the center, a tray of Martha Washington chocolates with mint filling, each topped with a pecan, a dish of chocolate fudge wrapped in wax paper, ginger snap cookies, a carafe of rich hot chocolate, and a fresh pot of coffee.

An egg timer on the counter went off. I looked through the oven window. The ham was done. Sliding on a pair of oven mitts, I opened the oven door and was blasted with an infernal heat. I lifted the pan with both hands and set it on a towel on the countertop. From the table, I fetched the empty serving platter and carefully transferred the ham over to it. The ham displayed beautifully, glazed with cloves and honey. Steam rose from the roasted meat.

At that moment, a gust of icy wind blew through the kitchen. The window in the back of the pantry was opened and swirls of snow had collected in a drift on the far wall near the shelves of canned vegetables. I ran over. The window was frozen and wouldn't budge. All my strength was not enough to close it. As I stood there, shivering, particles of sleet gathered on my cheeks and eyebrows, numbing them. My hands were trembling. Our backyard and patio were covered with steep drifts of snow. It was utterly dark except for a pinkish glow along the tree line.

While I tried to figure out a way to close the window, I

became aware of a sound coming from the hallway. It was someone crying. Though faint, it was a voice I recognized.

I gave up trying to close the window and went down the hallway. At last, I reached my mother's bedroom. Pressing my ear against the door, I listened. She was weeping inside. About what I do not know. All I could be sure of is that she was alone. I placed my hand upon the doorknob. Every part of me wanted to go inside, to make sure she was okay, but I couldn't bring myself to turn the knob. It wasn't in me. All I could do was listen from the hallway.

Standing there, I grew tired. All of a sudden, it became very difficult to keep my eyes open. I yawned, stretching my arms above my head, and continued down the hallway to my own bedroom, the one I shared with Rachel.

I was very careful not to make a sound as I pushed the door open and tiptoed across the hardwood floor. My sister was still asleep in her bed. I climbed into mine and nestled underneath the quilted blanket. I listened to the slurry of wind and snow pattering against the window, and soon fell back to sleep, dreaming of the day to come.

YMCA

To all parents:

 On Thursday, February 2nd, the YMCA After-school Program will be taking a field trip to the grand opening of the Bishop Science Museum to see the Dinosaurs of Northwest Georgia exhibition.

 If you would like your child to attend, please fill out the bottom portion of this form and return by Thursday, February 2nd, along with five dollars for the admission fee. Without the signed form and fee, your child WILL NOT BE ALLOWED to attend.

 Thank you!

It had been raining since morning, when my mother dropped me off at school. That was why I thought the field trip would be postponed. Nobody had said anything about it being postponed, so I'm not sure why I thought that, but I did. And that was why I left the permission slip, and the

1986

five-dollars admission fee, in my backpack upstairs. Mr. Leonard, our counselor, told me to run and fetch it so he could tally up the final headcount.

I bounded up the stairwell, ran across the basketball court, and pushed open the door to an unused locker room we called the bookbag room. The carpeted floor was strewn with backpacks, coats, and other school paraphernalia, most of it piled near the door. It was hard to see anything, since the fluorescent lights no longer worked. Usually, sunlight came in through narrow windows along the top of the walls, but on that day it was a somber and grayish light.

I tiptoed through the mess, looking for my bag. There was no telling where it was. I usually heaved the bag into the room from the doorway as a feat of strength. And the room was always cleared out by pickup time. But I did find it, eventually.

As I turned to leave, I saw something in the corner of my eye, and jumped.

There was a girl sitting on a bench under the window light. She was reading a library book. Her outfit was unusual. She was wearing an Alice Cooper t-shirt, faded blue jeans, and red Converse All-stars. Although I had been coming to the Afterschool Program for months, I couldn't remember ever seeing her before. And I would have remembered.

She gave no indication of having seen or heard me, which I found strange. But then she glanced up and my face immediately flushed. Her eyes were piercing, even in the half-light.

"Sorry," I said, sensing that I was interrupting her reading.

But she merely shrugged.

"It's fine."

Then she returned to her book.

Somehow, I couldn't bring myself to leave.

"I was just getting the permission slip from my bag."

She glanced up again, not annoyed exactly, but maybe a little impatient. "Okay."

"Are you going?" I asked, hoping to draw her into conversation.

"Going where?"

"To the museum."

"What museum?"

"The Bishop Science Museum," I said, and then added, "They have a dinosaur exhibit."

"Oh."

"It was in the newspaper last week."

"Oh," she repeated, and became quiet, as if she were far away, and then returned. "No, I'm not going to the museum."

Her gaze was fixed on the carpet, as if looking at something beyond it. As the moments ticked by, it became obvious she had forgotten I was even standing there. Then she picked up the library book and turned to the next page.

I took that as my cue to leave.

But I didn't.

When she glanced up again, I was expecting her piercing eyes, but I was not expecting her shy, and faintly embarrassed, smile.

"What's your favorite dinosaur?" she asked.

That was easy. "Tyrannosaurus rex."

She rolled her eyes a bit. "Boys always say that one."

I merely shrugged, and asked her the same question. She pondered, taking it seriously.

"I'd say a Brontosaurus."

"Nice, those are cool."

"I don't know," she added. "They seem gentle."

"Yeah, they do."

The locker room door opened, and a younger kid stood in the doorway, tossing his things on the floor. He jumped when he saw me standing there. He then peered around the room, met my stare briefly, before letting the door close on its own.

"Hey," she said, "wanna try this thing we learned in school?"

"Sure."

"Okay. First, you have to close your eyes."

"What, why?"

"Just trust me."

"Okay."

I closed my eyes, about to laugh.

"Why are you laughing?"

"I don't know," I said. "This is kind of weird."

"Be serious," she said, laughing too. "Now, I'm going to say a word and you have to tell me the first thing that pops into your head."
"Okay."
"Ready?"
"Yeah."
"Okay. Dinosaur."
I answered, lamely, "Tyrannosaurus rex."
"Food."
"Pepperoni Pizza."
"Dessert."
"Banana Split."
"Drink."
"Coca Cola."
"Mother."
"Uh, my mom."
And that was the end of it. When I opened my eyes, she was staring at me.
"Cool, huh?"
"I guess so."
"We learned about it in school."
"Learned what?"
"How your brain imprints a strong memory to a word, to help you learn. Like the word mother. That word will always be associated with your own mother. To you. Your whole life."
"That is pretty cool," I said. "I guess I never thought about it before."

1986

Neither of us seemed to know what to say. In the silence that followed, she averted her eyes from me, as if she had revealed something intimate about herself.

"You probably think I'm weird."

I began to understand why I had never seen her before. Why she was hiding out in the bookbag room instead of playing with the other children. I was overcome with an intense feeling of pity for her. In her face, I could see years of hurt, of isolation, of not belonging, and something in me wanted to take that hurt away, if it were possible.

"What's your name?"

She met my eyes and smiled.

"Angela."

I told her mine.

"It's nice to meet you," she said.

"It's nice to meet you too."

We both laughed.

A crack of thunder startled us both. It was followed by a rumble that shook the entire building. A sheet of rain slapped against the windows, and the room darkened.

Neither of us spoke. Angela flipped through the pages of the book. I stood there awkwardly. I felt like an idiot for not knowing what to say. Then I thought of something.

"Do you believe in ghosts?"

She seemed confused with the question, until I gestured towards the book in her hand.

"Oh, I don't know," she said. "Do you?"

I thought about it.

"Most of the time, I think ghosts are just a bunch of bull crap. Then other times, like in the middle of the night, or when I'm by myself, I'm not so sure anymore."

She gazed at the floor, thoughtful. "I'm the same way." Then she looked up, and her voice lowered to a whisper. "Did you know there's a ghost that haunts the Y?"

I had never heard that, and told her. She leaned forward, as if revealing a secret.

"Back in the seventies, a girl died in the basement."

"Whoa!"

"I know," she said. "Apparently, she was climbing on a shelf to reach softball equipment, and the whole thing collapsed on top of her."

"Really?"

"And since that time, a lot of people have seen her ghost, wandering the empty rooms of the building, looking for an exit. They say if you go down there, to the basement, you can sometimes hear her screaming. They say she's trapped and can never leave."

"Holy shit."

"I know."

"Is that why they keep the downstairs blocked off?"

She considered it.

"Well, I don't know why they keep it blocked off," she said, with an enigmatic smile, "but I know where the key is."

*

1986

We descended the stairwell. At the very bottom, piled in front of a door, was a stack of classroom desks. That made it nearly impossible to reach the door, much less to open it. I knew that from experience, as did every curious kid in the Afterschool Program.

In the same area, there was also a fire extinguisher mounted to the wall. Angela crawled underneath the extinguisher mount and fished her hand behind the bracket. A moment later she stood and held up a small brass key.

"How did you know that was there?"

She ignored my question and shimmied herself between the desks, squeezing into the small area in front of the door. She gestured for me to follow her, which I did with considerably more difficulty. When I had made it through, she handed me the key.

"You do it."

"Why me?"

She exhaled, seemingly annoyed.

"Not too late to turn back."

I couldn't tell what she meant by that. Did she want me to back out, or was she merely testing my courage? Regardless, I had to know what was on the other side of the door.

The key slid into the lock, and with a half turn, the deadbolt retracted.

I pushed against the door. It wouldn't budge. The hinges were rusted tight. In order to break the rust, it took us both shouldering against it. On the third shove, the door flung open. It smashed against the inside wall, and a reverberating boom echoed down a gloomy corridor.

We stepped through. The air was stale and gave off a mildewy stench. The walls of the corridor had once been painted white, but in the intervening years the paint had peeled off, like petals from a dying flower.

We passed by a break room and stopped to look around. Inside was a mustard yellow couch with tears in the cushions, a cigarette machine, and a rusty Frigidaire. Everything in the room was covered in dust, untouched by fingerprints.

Angela went to the refrigerator and opened it. I stood beside her. It was empty. A powerful sensation came over me. For a fraction of a moment, it felt like this was our refrigerator, in our home, twenty years into the future, when we were married with children, planning what to have for dinner on a Tuesday evening. We exchanged glances and left the break room to continue down the corridor.

At the end were two doors. The one to the left led into a locker room, and in the locker room, there was another door with a grimy window. Angela wiped it clean with her palm. On the other side of the door was a large pool room with broken skylight windows overhead. The pool was empty and filled with garbage. She turned the knob, but it was locked.

"Do you think the entrance to the basement is in there?"

"I don't know."

There was something in the corner of the pool room, hidden in the darkness. It was alive, that was sure. It appeared to be moving but was impossible to recognize from where we stood.

"What is that?"

"I have no idea."

"Let's not go in there."

"Great idea. Let's not."

The door to the right led into a gymnasium, not unlike the one upstairs, except the basketball hoops had been removed and the floor was covered with tarpaulin. Also, exactly in the middle of the court was an old van. It was a Dodge van, blue in color.

We walked around it, wiping the dust from the windows to see if anything was inside, but it was empty. However, the keys were in the ignition. The front bumper was also dented, and one headlight and the grill were broken, as if it had been in an accident.

"How in the world did this get down here?"

"I was wondering the same thing."

There didn't appear to be an entrance large enough to fit a van. That we could see. As we looked around, Angela pointed at a door near the restrooms. On the door was a sign.

BASEMENT: NOT AN EXIT

We approached the door and stood in front of it.

"Are you sure you want to go down there?" Angela asked.

I swallowed, but my mouth was dry.

"We don't have to," she added.

I'd be lying if I said there wasn't a part of me that wanted to turn back.

"No," I said. "Let's do it."

The stairway leading down was dark, but not so dark that we couldn't see. The stairs were wooden, unlike the ones in the rest of the building. The walls were exposed brick, and the air was cooler. I took the lead and held onto a handrail as I descended. After a few steps, I looked back and saw Angela's silhouette in the door frame. When she noticed I was waiting for me, she grabbed the handrail and followed.

The basement was an open space, with two windows on the longest wall. The windows, like everything else down there, were covered with years of dust and grime. Only the faintest light came through. In the corner sat an iron boiler, like some ancient mechanical altar, with a multitude of pipes, hatches, and gauges protruding from it. There were stacks of boxes and outdated gym equipment all piled on shelves and covered with cobwebs.

Angela had not spoken a word, but I could feel her standing next to me. As I stepped onto the basement floor, something crawled from the shadows. It scurried between our legs and disappeared under a workbench.

1986

We both startled, but Angela more than me. She took my hand, holding it tightly, and screamed with such abject terror that it curdled my blood.

Later that afternoon, our group of eleven children and Mr. Leonard was being led through the Dinosaurs of Northwest Georgia exhibit by a tour guide.

We stopped in front of a large placard, depicting a timeline back to the Proterozoic Eon, one billion years ago. She pointed out the top-most stratum of the timeline, called the Cenozoic Era. It was a thin green stripe meant to represent the age of mammals. The rest of the strata was illustrated with prehistoric flora and fauna. And dinosaurs of course.

The guide led us down a hallway, which opened into a series of connected rooms, each one filled with glass cases of fossils and other geologic artifacts. Minerals and rocks of various colors and shapes. Each room was larger than the previous. After the third room, one of the kids in our group asked the guide if we were ever going to see dinosaur bones or just dumb old rocks. Which is what we all were thinking. Everyone laughed.

"Ask and ye shall receive," the guide said.

We entered a room with only a single artifact. It was displayed in the center of the room, behind a red velvet rope. A fossilized Brontosaurus. We all crowded around the remnants of the ancient creature, mouths agape.

YMCA

A plaque hung from the velvet rope, etched with a description.

Brontosaurus (meaning "thunder lizard") is a genus of gigantic quadruped sauropod dinosaurs. It had a long, thin neck and a small head adapted for a herbivorous lifestyle, a bulky, heavy torso, and a long, whip-like tail. The various species lived during the Late Jurassic epoch, in the Morrison Formation of what is now North America, and were extinct by the end of the Jurassic. Adult individuals of Brontosaurus are estimated to have measured up to 19–22 meters (62–72 feet) long and weighed up to 14–17 tonnes (15–19 short tons).

I imagined what the Brontosaurus must have been like when it was alive. The sheer enormity of it, trudging through the same valley where our town stood, at the foothills of the Appalachians, munching on treetops. I imagined its family, mother and father, grandparents, siblings. Did it ever swim through rivers? Or watch the sunset over a mountain peak? Did it ever wonder about a time millions of years into the future, when human children would gaze upon its fossilized bones in a museum, surrounded by a velvet rope, with a plaque that was necessary to explain what it once had been?

When I emerged from my daydream, I was surprised to see my group had already exited for the next room. It was just me and the Brontosaurus. As I departed to rejoin the tour, my footsteps echoed off the high walls and polished, concrete floors.

On the drive back, there was traffic. It was from the bad weather, Mr. Leonard said. He had one eye on the road, and the other on us kids. We were cutting up in the back of the van, hooting and hollering, tossing balls of wadded paper, and making a general ruckus.

"Hey y'all," Mr. Leonard said, checking the side mirrors before merging into an open lane. "Quiet down back there, or I'm gonna write a note to y'all's parents. I'm serious now!"

He was having a hard time driving in the rain. It was obvious he was not used to such a large vehicle, veering outside the lines and misjudging how soon to brake at traffic lights. The noise we were making wasn't helping the situation at all.

We came around a curve to an intersection. Mr. Leonard had not seen that the light was yellow, and the van was going too fast. The cars ahead had slowed down, their brake lights reflecting in the tiny raindrops on the windshield. Our tires skidded on the wet asphalt. Mr. Leonard shouted over his shoulder.

"Hold on guys, we're gonna hit em!"

The impact flung me against the seat ahead. My wrist buckled under the force, and I banged my head, causing me to see stars.

Thankfully, nobody was badly hurt. Our van took the

bulk of the damage. And the bumper of the station wagon we hit from behind.

After the police arrived on scene, Mr. Leonard called the YMCA. They sent another van to pick us up, but we had to sit in the wrecked van until the other one arrived. As we waited, all there was to do was watch the police officer, Mr. Leonard, and the woman in the station wagon stand outside in the rain and discuss the accident. There were blue lights flashing on the police car, and traffic going around us.

My mother was upset. By the time we arrived, she was already waiting in the lobby of the YMCA. Afterwards, we picked up Rachel from the babysitter, and drove to the Piggly Wiggly for groceries. The entire time she was prodding me with questions, wanting to know exactly what happened, where I was hurt, and debating whether to take me to the emergency room for x-rays. I kept insisting I was okay, but she was not hearing it. The more it went on, the angrier she became.

Walking the frozen aisle at the grocery store, she handed me a bag of peas to soothe the lump that had appeared on my forehead. Rachel got mad that I had a bag of peas while she didn't, and she began crying. So my mother gave her a bag of peas too, which she placed on her forehead, copying me.

"One thing is for sure," my mother said, while picking out a gallon of milk, "you're never going back to the YMCA. Not after this."

1986

I defended Mr. Leonard, saying it was just an accident, but it was useless.

"But I like it there," I said. "Where else am I gonna go?"

My mother shrugged.

"I haven't figured that out yet, son. Maybe you can stay with Miss Judy."

I huffed. "Only babies stay there. The Y is fun. There's kids my age."

The discussion was over. We checked out, put the groceries in the back of the station wagon, and drove home. Back home, my mother prepared supper for us, while I spent the rest of the evening on the couch, holding an ice pack over my injuries, watching television.

As for Angela, shy and pretty and not weird, the one who would always be Angela to me, we never met again.

2006

A wave breaks on the shore and washes over our feet. As it recedes, a slurry of water and sand filters through the gaps between our toes. She glances at me, pensive, and asks if the buildings are still on fire. Behind us, at a great distance, an orange haze rises from a jagged line of flames. I tell her what I see. She goes quiet. Another moment passes and I remind her I should be going soon. She knows I am headed to the airport. We embrace. She whispers in my ear that she has always loved me and always will. Then she takes my hand and leads me to a blanket. We collapse, holding onto one another, and kiss. I make my way to her neck, brushing aside locks of her auburn hair. I focus on details, the mole on her nape, the scent of lotion, the faded graphic on the t-shirt she is wearing, Welcome to My Nightmare. I place my hand under her shirt and lift it up, exposing her belly. Lost in reverie, the moment passes like a hundred years. Her eyes have been closed, but now open, beholding something in the night sky. She rises, me watching her, watching the sky. Her eyes are wet with tears. I ask her what's the matter. She says, "it's a full moon!" and points with a delicate finger. I follow the gesture and see it for myself, gargantuan wings fluttering among the stars. Antenna, thorax, abdomen, pocked with craters, and shining a pale cerulean. The rhythmic beating of its wings has stirred up the tide. The seas whitecap to the horizon, presaging a storm yet to come. I can tell she is afraid. So am I, but I won't admit it. "Maybe we'd better go," she says. And before I can respond, we are swallowed by a rogue wave crashing onto the beach. As we are tossed and twirled, I desperately hold onto her hand. She squeezes back, as if to say, don't let me go, no matter what. In the chaos it is impossible to tell which way is up. The wave recedes and we are still on the beach, holding hands. I ask if she is okay and get no response. I notice her hand feels different now. There is a dawning realization that something awful has happened. In the moonlight, I feel her body. It has become a globular mass of flesh, vaguely serpentine in form. My mouth opens to scream, but the sheer horror of it prevents me from vocalizing. Her skin is scaly, covered in a thin layer of mucous. At the head, there are tusks growing from a grotesquely enlarged mouth. In disgust, I attempt to let go of her hand, resembling a fin, but I cannot. At the head, a cyclopean yellow eye opens and slowly blinks. The mouth dilates and pink, toothy insides fountain outward and envelop me. The esophagus undulates, pushing me deeper into its digestive system. Panic-stricken, I flail against the tunnel of flesh, but I have no leverage, being squeezed from all sides. I look around but can't even tell if my eyes are open anymore, because there is nothing to see except a black void. I begin to comprehend the futility of my situation and turn docile. Outside, I sense movement and imagine that another wave must have come and dragged the creature back into the ocean. Despite my reality, I feel a sense of calm emanate from within. My eyes become accustomed to the darkness. I am somehow able to see through the innards of my devourer. Through its skin. I glimpse the depths which engulf us both. There are no rough seas or currents down here. There is life, however. Unusual creatures that have never witnessed sunlight, existing somewhere in the hypnagogia of classification. I see natural formations of rock and primeval calcifications rising from bottomless fathoms, miles below, where no human being has ever been. It occurs to me that I will soon run out of oxygen. I turn away from the outer world and contemplate my helplessness. How far I am from the airport, I laugh. How ridiculous that hope was, to believe I would ever make it there. But I let it go. I let everything go. My plans for the future. My responsibilities. An inner voice reminds me of something I have always known, but never acknowledged in the world above. Nothing is left undone. I repeat the words over and over, like a mantra. With every breath I take, the darkness encroaches. I allow it to happen. I even want it to happen. My thoughts turn to my family and friends and colleagues. All those relationships that meant so much to me. When I think of my mother, I am filled with sorrow. Not for my sake, but for hers. She will be the one to miss me the most. And like any good son, I never want to cause her pain. But then, I realize, even if my death causes her pain, even that is temporary and not something to be avoided. You lived a good life. You tried to do good. To be a good person. And to leave your insignificant corner of the universe better than you found it. And even if you didn't always succeed, it was enough to try. Nothing is lost, and nothing is left undone. Then, all the world goes dark for me. Time passes in silent contemplation. But soon, a disturbance. The muffled sloshing of ocean waves. I open my eyes, and a brilliant light pierces the void. Then human voices. I escape from a wound that has been cut into the side of the creature. A man is towering over me. He has a full beard and is wearing rain gear. Others surround him, but I cannot make out their faces. I am standing on the back deck of a work boat, amidst the tidal storm. The deck is illuminated with halogen flood lights. The man with the full beard is the first mate. He is growling at me. He points at my bare feet, berating me for not wearing my safety boots. The phone rings and one of the crewmen rushes over to answer it. He hangs up and whispers into the ear of the first mate, who nods. The first mate scowls and informs me that the captain needs coffee. I stumble through the hatch into the galley. The pot of coffee is freshly brewed, sloshing along with the motion of the vessel. I pour a steel decanter, along with milk and two dollops of honey. Then I proceed up the stairway to the wheelhouse, bracing myself whenever the boat lurches. The wheelhouse is dark inside, lit with dim, red lights. I approach the captain, sitting at the helm. A frail hand reaches out. His hair is long and straggly, his peacoat mildewed and covered with strands of seaweed. I try to make eye contact with him, but his face is obscured in shadows. I look out the front windows, just as the vessel crests an enormous wave. The bow tips over a drop of ten stories. I am overcome with vertigo. As we descend, my stomach tries to escape through my mouth. I feel as weightless as a dove. At the trough of the wave, a swell of ocean water comes over the bow and smashes against the wheelhouse. The force of it shatters the windows, and a cascade floods in. Somehow, I am washed onto the back deck again. The vessel loses power and drifts parallel to the seas. We're going to capsize, I think. The first mate runs up to me. He looks like a drowning victim, his face bloated and his skin sallow. He gestures towards land off the starboard side, a half mile away. There is a port with amber lights, cranes, and warehouses. Somehow, we make it dockside. I look at my watch and see that it's nearly daylight. That means crew change. The sky has turned the color of steel, which I recognize to be the coming of dawn. I don my hard hat and walk the gangway to the dock. I head to the parking lot, a duffle bag slung over my shoulder. All the vehicles are covered in dust, which makes it

1986

hard to tell which car is mine in the predawn light. I somehow locate my Jeep. I wipe the windows with an old towel, toss my bag into the passenger seat, and take off down the road. The longer I drive, the more difficult it becomes to see out the windows. I pull over a couple times to clean off the dust. No matter what I do, the windows just won't come clean. I soon enter a small town and recall someone telling me about a car wash here. On both sides of the road there are shuttered storefronts and dilapidated buildings. Tufts of grass protrude from cracks in the sidewalk. Further down, I notice the buildings are bathed in flashing, rainbow lights. I roll down the window and listen. There are sounds of people. I drive towards it, round the corner, and discover the car wash. It is a welcome sight. The entire building is outlined in yellow neon lights. There is a gigantic clown face in blue and red around the mouth of the autowash entrance. A crowd of people sit outside on benches, talking and laughing. None of them seem to notice me. I pull up to the autowash and insert five dollars into a machine. The security bar lifts, and I pull onto the tracks. The lights on the machinery inside start blinking and circus music begins to play over a cheap loudspeaker. When the conveyor fires up, my vehicle lurches forward. Aluminum nozzles pivot downward and spray from side to side, soaking my vehicle in a purple, watery soap. Overhead, a mechanism of bristles comes to life, spinning. It descends slowly, but just as it reaches the front grille, a hose comes loose, spraying water. There is a violent rattle.

Metal grinding. The wheel of bristles comes to an abrupt stop. The brackets holding the wheel shear off, and the whole structure crashes onto my hood. Shrapnel flies everywhere. Metal fragments shatter the lights. The autowash tunnel goes dark. The music stops. I open the door, stepping onto broken glass. Unsure what to do next, I walk outside and notice the entire car wash is abandoned. It looks as if it's been out of business for years. The people are gone. I am overcome with a feeling of hopelessness. There is nothing to do but run. But a few blocks later, I need to stop and catch my breath. In the back of my mind, I wonder if the car wash was a dream. And for the briefest of moments, it occurs to me that all of this could merely be a dream I am having. But it passes. I am lost, at night, in the middle of some forgotten rural town on the backroads of Acadiana. There is somewhere I needed to be. I know that much, but I can't remember where, or even why it was important to begin with. I only know that it is gone. The need is gone. There is a maze-like quality to the streets. Each block resembles the next. Each corner and intersection the same. I choose a direction and run. Not for any reason, only a vague feeling that I need to get out of here. After several minutes of running, the only thing that has changed is the sky. It is now the faintest blue, mixed with shades of pink. After stopping to rest—only for a moment—I double-back the way I came. As I round a familiar corner, something is changed. There is a vacant lot the span of an entire block surrounded by construction barriers. Between the partitions, there is an opening. I walk over and peer inside. There is a chain-link fence and a yellow sign over an entryway. The sign is obscure. It's not that I can't understand the language, or even decipher the individual words on it, but the overall message eludes me. Like sitting in the front row at a movie theater. I can't get enough perspective. Beyond the fence is a field of tall grass, as high as a person. Something about this place feels different from the town. I can't describe the feeling exactly, but I desperately want to get inside. The latch on the gate is unlocked, so I enter and head into the tall grass. The ground is muddy. My feet sink into it. After some time, I trip over a tree root, and come upon a large oak tree. I recognize it. When I was ten years old, I used to climb up the same tree and hang from its branches. A concrete path leads to the front door. A holly bush grows in front of a bay window, the same window through which I once accidentally kicked a soccer ball. I walk up the front porch steps and turn the doorknob. It is open. The living room is decorated with strands of blinking Christmas lights. There is a small tree on a table, hung with bells and tinsel. The floor is almost entirely covered with opened boxes and torn wrapping paper. The only thing missing are the gifts themselves. And my family. I head into the kitchen and see the remnants of a feast, with empty dishes and used plates with forks and knives sitting on top. Then I hear a muffled jangle of bells coming from the basement. The door to the basement squeaks, so I am very careful

2006

not to make a sound when I turn the knob. I creep downstairs, hand on the rail, pausing on each step, to minimize the creaking. At the bottom of the stairs, I pass a small window and a glint of morning sunlight blinds me temporarily. As I peer into the basement, I see a man sitting at my grandfather's workbench, his back to me. He is focused on a task of great importance. With some trepidation, I step closer. He appears to be wearing my grandfather's clothes. His western shirt, his cowboy boots. I am only a few feet away from him. As of yet unseen. This emboldens me, so I enter his periphery, but he still doesn't seem to notice, or care, that I am standing there. His eyes are fixed intently on his work. He is a young man, about my age. There is something else in his eyes besides the determination. A lack of worry. The presence of hope. Everything is ahead of him, this man wearing my grandfather's clothes. He has an entire lifetime to anticipate, and nothing, as of yet, to regret—

The phone rang from the living room. After our fight, I knew Suzanne wouldn't bother to answer. I rolled off the futon in the computer room, hoping to catch it before the machine.

"Hello?" I said, yawning.

It was my mother's voice. The last time we spoke was months ago. She asked me how I was doing. All that. Even before she said anything, I could tell something was wrong. Normally, she wouldn't have called so early in the morning. Especially on a weekday. I told her I was fine, and asked how she was doing. Waiting for it. After the pleasantries, her voice lowered.

"Well," she said, "I was calling to let you know your grandfather passed away. In his sleep, they said. So, peacefully at least. I don't know all the details yet. But there will be a service at the hospital chapel in Milledgeville. Don't feel like you have to come. I know it's a long drive."

The following morning, Suzanne and I had still not talked. She had been hiding out in our bedroom, door closed, while I had stayed on the computer, mindlessly surfing the web.

I was in the living room, memorizing the directions I had printed out. Our bedroom door opened and she walked out wearing those bug-eyed sunglasses, with a beach bag draped over her arm. She noticed that I was dressed formally.

"Where are you going?"

I told her about the funeral.

She hugged me tenderly, and asked if there was anything she could do.

"Not really."

Then she left to meet her friend Michelle on the boardwalk.

My bag was packed. There was still time to kill before I needed to get on the road. I made a pot of coffee and sat on the couch. While I sipped, I glanced around the apartment. The sparse furniture. The white walls. On the floor, in the corner of the dining room, was broken glass and a pool of coagulated red wine, still untouched from that night.

The problem was that I didn't love Suzanne. Not really. Nor did she love me. Really. I had no delusions about it. Or maybe I did. I guess I did. The thing is, we had been perfect together for a singular moment in space and time. Our orbits crossed, two planets spiraling into a black hole, each as lost as the other, and that had been enough to keep us from drifting apart for a while. But the gravitational pull that had brought us together was weakening. Our connection was dying. I resented her for that, even though it was at least half my fault. I knew she resented me too. At the time, neither of us were strong enough to make the choice to be alone. Though eventually, she was the one.

I got on the road.

Before merging onto the interstate, I stopped at a gas station near the exit to fill up the Cherokee and get snacks. In the passenger seat were the directions. Every chance I got I studied the turns ahead. It was a six-hour drive to Milledgeville, and I knew I'd be cutting it close.

The weather was overcast, with intermittent rays of sunshine coming through the clouds. At least it wasn't raining yet. The forecast had said there might be rain.

As I drove, the featureless landscape of the Florida panhandle gave way to the rolling hills of southern Georgia. I listened to the radio for a while, but it started to

1986

annoy me, so I turned it off. The silence allowed me to think.

Somewhere outside Macon I got turned around. Because I wasn't paying attention to the road. I only realized my mistake when I saw a sign that said Gainesville 287 miles. So at the next exit I pulled into a Hardees and studied the directions. It was impossible to know where I had turned wrong. I needed a road map of Georgia.

I got back on the road and found the nearest gas station. The whole time, I avoided looking at the clock on the dashboard, because I knew it'd only make me more anxious. There was no question about it. I hadn't given myself enough time. I was going to be late. The only question was by how much. I was fuming. Cursing myself for not paying attention.

When I saw the Welcome to Milledgeville sign, I finally glanced at the radio clock. The service had already begun. I sped through the next few traffic lights, weaving through cars, until I saw a sign for the state hospital.

Pulling into the parking lot, I recognized the chapel steeple rising above the institutional buildings. I found a spot and ran-walked to the chapel entrance, where an usher greeted me. He handed me a program and gestured inside.

The chapel was smaller than it looked from the outside. Its walls were paneled with dark-lacquered woodwork. In front, there was an ornate altar over which hung a burnished bronze cross, surrounded by carven angels. The casket lay below the altar, its lid closed. The pews were mostly empty, except for the front row. My family was sitting there. I took a seat in the back row to not make a scene. Somewhere an organ was playing The Old Rugged Cross. As the final notes of the hymn faded away, the pastor approached the lectern and gave everyone a beneficent smile. He opened the Bible and began reading aloud.

"First Corinthians, chapter fifteen, verse forty-two has something to say about death. Behold, it begins, I show you a mystery. We shall not all sleep, but we shall all be changed. In a moment, in the twinkling of an eye, at the last trump. For the trumpet shall sound, and the dead shall be raised incorruptible, and we shall be changed. For this corruptible must put on incorruption, and this mortal must put on immortality. So when this corruptible shall have put on incorruption, and this mortal shall have put on immortality, then shall be brought to pass the saying that is written, Death is swallowed up in victory. O death, where is thy sting? O grave, where is thy victory? The sting of death is sin. And the strength of sin is the law. But thanks be to God, which giveth us the victory through our Lord Jesus Christ."

The pastor closed the book. He welcomed our family and told the story of visiting my grandfather in the hospital during his final hours. Praying with him.

"He confessed to me, when nobody else was in the room, that he had never been a religious man. In fact, he said, he had often been a sinner. Well, aren't we all, ladies and gentlemen? So it was my profound honor as a servant of Christ to tell him the good news. Yes siree. The news being that it does not matter to the Lord if you were a sinner, or are a sinner, or will be a sinner, just as long as you have accepted Him into your heart. Truly. For the Lord knows your heart, and the contents therein, and remembers you forever. You can be sure of that, my friends. You will not be forgotten at the end of days, when the Lord in Heaven returns for every son and daughter. Because to be forgotten is what the world wants, not our Creator."

There were nods and amens from the ushers standing by the exits. The pastor went on to explain how my grandfather finally accepted Jesus into his heart, and thus secured his place in Heaven. Looking at the pastor, with his pudgy, ruddy face, his helmet hair, I became incensed. None of this had anything to do with my grandfather. Nothing to honor the man he was in life. I wanted to stand up and tell them all to fuck right off.

But I didn't.

When the service ended, an usher opened the side door, letting in rays of hazy light. The organ played The Old Rugged Cross again. My family stood up and filed out the door. I thought one of them might glance back to see if I was there, but no one did.

The pastor asked everyone else in attendance to follow the family to the burial site. I rose with the others and walked down the center aisle, pausing at the casket. One of the ushers noticed me standing there and raised the lid.

2006

I did not recognize the person inside. It was a frail, wasted body, wearing an ill-fitted suit. The hair was parted neatly on the side, in a way he had never worn it in life. The face was caked with makeup, stopping below the hairline, which revealed the waxy and pale skin underneath. It could not be the same man I had known. For one, my grandfather had never been so—

A tear fell onto my cheek. I wiped it away and nodded to the usher. He closed the lid, and I went out the door to join my family at the burial site.

They were all standing in the area reserved by a sign. My mother, Rachel, her husband Brandon, and their little girl Madison, who I had only seen once at Christmastime three years ago when she was just born. My father was also there, which was a surprise to me. I had not spoken to him in years. Everyone was just like I remembered them. Maybe a bit grayer, a bit fatter, but the same.

I approached from behind and hugged my mother. She gasped when she recognized me and gave me a long hug in return. Everyone else greeted me with smiles. My mother thanked me for coming, saying she thought I wouldn't be able to make it because of work.

"Of course I made it," I said. "He was my grandpa."

My mother nodded and stared at the grave.

"He was a hard man, from a different time. We didn't always see eye to eye, and he wasn't always the best father to me, but was my daddy, and I loved him."

A few minutes later, we saw them exit a large door with

four ushers acting as pallbearers. By then it had begun to drizzle, and there was a mist gathering at the edge of the cemetery grounds. My mother and sister pulled umbrellas from their purses. The rest of us stood in the rain, our heads bowed.

After the funeral, we met at a buffet next to the highway.

The waitress seated us, taking our drink orders. We piled food on our plates and ate together. The conversation was reserved. My father started talking with Brandon about the football game, and I tuned out. There was another family sitting across from us. I watched them for a while. They were laughing and carrying on.

Despite not being all that hungry, I was already on my second plate, thinking about what to have for dessert. Rachel waved a fork in front of my face.

"Sorry," I said. "Just daydreaming."

I felt everyone looking at me.

"No, you're good. I was just telling mom that me and Brandon are thinking about getting a puppy for Madison. Because every kid ought to have a pet. Like, I was telling him on the drive over about the dog we grew up with. Ol' Graham. You remember him?"

"Of course I do. Best dog I ever had."

The conversation turned to Rachel's new job. She was working as a cashier at Dollar General. I was feeling somewhat guilty about not being fully present at the table, so I made an effort and asked how she was liking it so far.

She shrugged. "I mean, it helps to pay the bills."

She asked me about life offshore.

"It's going okay," I answered. "The pay is good, but someday I want to find a decent-paying job on land."

She laughed.

"Heck, you and me both!"

I pointed at Madison, who was sitting in a booster seat, playing with her chicken nuggets.

"She sure has grown. Last time I saw her she was just a baby."

"I know it," Rachel said. "We don't ever get to see you anymore."

"I know."

"Who do you think Madison favors more, me or Brandon?"

I thought about it.

"She definitely favors you in the eyes. But I do see Brandon around the mouth."

"Brandon always says her mouth must come from me, because she's so loud."

Everyone laughed.

"I just meant her physical features."

"I know," she said, patting me on the back. "I was just teasing."

Neither of us knew where to take the conversation after that, so we stared down at our plates. Madison began crying. Rachel leaned over to check her diaper and saw that it needed changing. She got up and walked to the restroom, her kid dangling from one arm, and a diaper bag on the other.

Our waitress arrived just as Rachel left. She had a pitcher of sweet tea and filled our glasses. My father stopped her before she filled his glass, informing her he couldn't have sweet tea anymore. He had to drink unsweetened tea, because of his diabetes. The waitress nodded and said she'd be right back with the other pitcher. My father turned to me.

"How you been, stranger? Don't hear from you no more."

"Phone works both ways, Daddy."

He nodded, half-smiling.

"That's true," he said. "I guess it does."

He told me he had just gotten out of the hospital. Kidney stones.

"Damn, I'm sorry to hear that. Was it painful?"

"Oh yes. I was telling your mama, now I know what childbirth feels like."

I chuckled.

"I heard that."

There was a lull. Then I thought of something to ask about.

"You been going to any car shows lately?"

He shook his head. "Ain't fun no more."

"Why's that?"

"I don't know. It just got old."

"Yeah, I hear you."

While I was talking with my father, Rachel and Madison had returned, and she was gossiping with my mother about someone I didn't know. My mother noticed the lull in our conversation and got my attention.

"Do you remember a boy named Noah Blankenship? You and him used to ride bikes when we lived with Nana and Grandpa. Down the road."

I tried to recall someone by that name but drew a blank.

"Can't say I remember a Noah."

"Oh," she said, somewhat confused. "I was going to say, he died last week. Got in a bar fight down in Rockmart. Didn't even make it to the hospital, they said. Stabbed in the liver."

"Mama," Rachel said.

"What? That's what I heard."

"Still, you don't have to be so gruesome."

"You really don't remember him? At one time y'all was close friends."

"I really don't."

"That's sad."

"Too young," Rachel said. "I wonder if he had kids of his own."

Nobody said much after that. It seemed we had run out of things to say. Everybody just picked at their plates and made small talk.

1986

My family was sitting no more than an arm's length away, but it may as well have been a million miles. I felt like a stranger to them. And they felt like strangers to me. I was overcome with an unbearable sadness, of loss, of a world I had always known, slipping through my fingers, and being helpless to catch it.

My father and sister had begun arguing about politics and the war in Iraq. Before I even realized what was happening, I was interrupting them. Talking about the dream I had. The night before. Every detail I remembered of it. All the strange things leading up to meeting my grandfather as a young man in the basement of that old house in Sherwood Forest. As I spoke, the restaurant seemed to disappear. The buffet, the dining room, the other patrons. Vanished. All that remained was us.

The table fell silent. Nobody said anything at first. I began to feel guilty. Like I was being selfish. Like I was making the day about myself. I glanced up, and everyone was staring at me. At the other end of the table, there were tears welling my mother's eyes.

Then she told us about her dream. From the night before. My grandfather, her father, had apparently visited her too. She described the dream to us, what she had seen, how she felt, and her reaction when the hospital called the next morning to let her know he had passed.

My sister clutched her chest.

"What in the world?"

She placed her hand upon my mother's hand.

"Oh, Mama," she said. "I had a dream about Grandpa too!"

My sister described her own dream to us.

And when she had finished, my father let us know he had also been visited. He couldn't remember the exact details but was sure that it happened.

Nobody knew what to say, after that. We were dumbstruck.

The dining room returned. I looked around and wondered how the other patrons in the restaurant could sit there eating, as if a miracle had not just occurred.

My family sat in silence. Every once in a while one of us would say something, not addressing the table, but giving a voice to things we were all feeling.

"I thought I was alone."

"I just don't understand anything about this world. I really don't."

"I swear, the longer I live, the less I seem to know."

"It could just be a weird coincidence, is all I'm saying."

"Hush, Brandon," Rachel said. "You don't know everything there is."

"I just hope we don't forget one day. That it really happened."

"We might, if we don't take care to remember."

"That's what the world wants."

"Amen."

"I won't ever forget. I know I won't."

"Me neither."

1986

"I would have said something sooner," my father confessed, "but I didn't want you guys to think I was crazy."

There was a pause. Then my mother said under her breath, just loud enough for everyone to hear, "You're about ten years too late for that."

It was so unexpected, everyone burst into laughter. Even my father had to laugh.

"That was good!" he said. A tear ran down the side of his face, "Lord, I needed that."

Then, as the laughter died out, my father broke into an uncontrollable sob. He tried to stifle it, to no avail.

"I just love y'all to death!" he said. "Each and every one of you guys means the world to me." Then, wiping his eyes. "I'm sorry for that y'all. I don't know what I'm saying."

Rachel reached across the table and took my father by the hand.

"Aw, Daddy. You don't have to apologize. Look, now you got me crying."

My mother dried her eyes and sighed.

"It's so easy to let life get in the way. Maybe we don't spend enough time together. We should make time for each other while we're still here."

We all agreed and promised that we would.

The waitress brought our check. We paid the bill and went outside the restaurant. The sun was low on the horizon and the ghost of a crescent moon was rising in the eastern sky. My sister pulled out a digital camera and took a group photo of us. Then we all hugged and said we'd be in touch.

One by one, our vehicles pulled out of the parking lot, merging into the endless flow of traffic, each going its own direction.

ACKNOWLEDGMENTS

The book you are reading would not exist if not for the following people:

My family, who unwittingly provided much source material for these fictional stories: Nana and Grandpa, Maw Maw and Paw Paw, Mama, Daddy, Arien, Grey, and Sydney. And of course Birch, my son, for the joy of witnessing his brotherly interactions (and fussing and fighting) with sister Zinnia.

Ita Salas, my friend and artist, whose dedication to painting was a constant source of inspiration during moments of doubt.

Rebecca Roland, whose steady friendship and support helped me through both good times and bad.

Dave Haynes, my longest friend, whose funny and reflective short stories about growing up in a small town directly inspired this book.

My childhood friends Kenneth Taylor, Chuck Waldron, and several others whose names I cannot recall anymore, though I do remember them.

Brad Watson, the great writer from Mississippi, whose class I snuck into as a poor undergrad student, who taught me that "good writing is always a little bit stupid" – a paradoxical nugget of wisdom I carry with me to this day.

Nicole Fegan and Steven Genise, whose thoughtful and thorough editorial notes helped elevate this book to its full potential.

Euan Monaghan, who designed the beautiful interior.

Thank you all.

Will Stepp lives and
writes in Rome, Georgia.

willstepp.com